FIRST FICTION

G.A. Cuddy

Printed in the United States of America

First Printing, 2015

ISBN-13: 978-1512324389

Representation

Christian Schraga
STA Literary Agency
staliterary.com

Social Media

@First_Fiction
@STALiterary

For Carrie

CHAPTER ONE

Ingrid Fallon's greatest fear was of not leaving an impression upon the world.

As a child, she would spin around her family's living room like a ballerina doing the 32 continuous fouettés from *Swan Lake* until she would get dizzy and crash into a pile of books nearby. Ingrid's home was an obstacle course of cultural literacy so it would be impossible for anyone to perform such daredevil maneuvers without running into something. There were crossword puzzles littering the floors, encyclopedia volumes topped kitchen counters, and travel magazines could be found under beds and stacked untidily in the garage.

Of her earliest memories, Ingrid could most vividly recall the feel of *National Geographic* issues rolled up with frayed edges that had been warped from the steam of showers, baths, and sultry summers in Louisiana. Each room of the house was like a library unto itself with the biographies of poets, painters, and politicians flanking the classics of fiction. Ingrid would plop herself down onto a comfortable chair or couch and be at an arm's length from the rest of the world. And, to verify the locations of the many far-off lands she hoped to visit, she kept both a globe and an atlas atop the desk in her room. Ingrid was raised to be inquisitive and to possess a view of the world far beyond the boundaries of her lily-speckled yard.

She grew up like many girls in Shreveport who were white, upper-middle class, and lived on the shade tree-lined streets in the neighborhood of South Highlands. Ingrid's father was a college professor and her mother was an elementary school teacher. Seamus Fallon had met the energetic Kathleen O'Connor when he was a lieutenant in the Air Force and she was a senior in college at Furman in South Carolina. Theirs was, for the most part, a typical military courtship. They corresponded with long letters when Seamus was stationed overseas and soon found that, in addition to the strong attraction they had upon first meeting, their mutual affection for words, language, diction, grammar, spelling, and literature formed a sincere bond of love.

He constructed crossword puzzles for her, then she would solve them and send originals of her own back to him. They got married a month before John F. Kennedy was assassinated in Dallas and Ingrid was born two years later. Seamus never spoke of his time in Vietnam.

The Fallons lived on Erie Street, directly across from an elementary school and less than ten blocks from Ingrid's all-girls Catholic high school, St. Vincent's Academy. Their home was airy and open, much like the minds of Ingrid's parents. Seamus was born in Belfast, Northern Ireland. He had traveled to the United States to attend college and play soccer. Seamus also knew that a commission in the Air Force meant he could become a citizen of the United States.

There was large map of the world on a wall near the kitchen table. Each family member had a pin color to mark his or her travels. Green was for Seamus, orange for Kathleen. Ingrid's sister, Moira, used blue to denote her eleven years of destinations. White, like the color of the Irish lilies growing at the foot of pine trees in their yard, was reserved for Ingrid. The planet seemed to be green and orange to the girls with just a few speckles of blue and white. They often joked that, one day, the map would disintegrate because of all of the pinholes. Their goal was to help accomplish this by trips of their own over the course of their lives.

At fifteen, about to turn sixteen in the summer of 1981, Ingrid was the typical aloof teenager attending St. Vincent's. She was the type of young woman that parents and grandparents found strikingly attractive, yet one that boys in her age range for dating at nearby Jesuit High School certainly overlooked. St. Vincent's Academy, shortened to SVA by locals, had a dress code of grey skirts, light blue buttoned tops, white socks, and Saddle Oxford shoes. There was little space for individuality or self-expression with strict nuns patrolling the hallways for uniform violations. Similarly, there was little room for any form of creative expression outside of regimented art classes and choral groups.

It seemed that Ingrid was living two lives. One, at home, was a vibrant roundtable of breakfast discussions about articles read aloud from *The New York Times*, debates concerning the meanings of poems by Keats and Yeats, and daily quizzes about current events. At school, Ingrid seemed locked into a rudimentary world of standardized education that St. Vincent's proclaimed superior to the local public schools because of its religious foundation. Her subtle defiance appeared in anonymous editorials she penned for the school paper, as well her involvement with cross-country running. Her father, a competitive athlete in high school and college, had fostered a love for the sport with Ingrid. She took to it well and, with a genetic predisposition for endurance, loved going on solitary early morning runs through South Highlands.

Though many might consider her quiet and calm, Ingrid's inner fire burned when she was able to pass adults on the predawn jogs with her father. She would play a game with herself by sneaking up on the older runners and then blowing past them with a sprint. Ingrid often wondered if they knew who she was, or how old she was, or whether they even knew that she was a teenage girl. She kept a count in her head of how many people she passed and would record it in a corner of her word-of-the-day desk calendar. In her bedroom after these runs, she would recover with a large glass of water while stretching in front of a mirror. She felt as satisfied by her good workouts as she did earning a perfect score on a geometry test.

Her body was changing. She had once considered herself malformed and uncoordinated, but now she was elongating. A womanly, fit shape was emerging. Ingrid's legs were strong and lean. Her torso was lithe and her dark hair fell upon shoulders that were alabaster in color when she was at rest, but a nearly maddening red when engaged in physical activity. Her skin was clear and clean, freckles dotted her graceful nose, and her robust lips appeared to leap off her face. A mother's mix of Greek, Italian, and Irish heritage coupled with a father's Irish lineage had produced a beautiful swan, but one still camouflaged at the time by the hierarchy of high school social caste systems of coolness. She was the type of girl that no one notices until it is too late for them to have a chance, like one that magically appears at a ten-year reunion and glides into a ballroom to gawks and stares from fattened, miserable admirers. Ingrid was intelligent, athletic, culturally-literate, and attractive. And no one in Shreveport or anywhere else in the world at the time recognized it if their last name was not Fallon.

Ingrid also kept a secret from that world. It was not something that she could tell her parents about, or tell her best friend Laura Wheeler, or even write in the diary that she kept tucked between her mattress and bed frame. She had started keeping notes on her daily activities when she was in third grade and now, near the end of her sophomore year of high school, she had nearly eight school terms of collected thoughts, memories, and original poems. It made sense that she found her releases in writing and running.

These were activities that she could do alone, without outside interference, when she needed the solitude that the whirlwinds of both her home and school could never provide. Ingrid thought about her secret when she ran by herself, but she never told a soul what it was. Most of the time, she preferred to run with her father and not alone.

Attending SVA was like being inside of a cocoon that was inside of another cocoon protected by crucifixes, images of Jesus and the Virgin Mary on the walls, and statues of various saints. Like its brother school of Jesuit, there were a few hundred students and they all lived in Shreveport neighborhoods that were mostly affluent and white. There were three African-American girls at St. Vincent's and their presence went as unnoticed as three girls of their same skin color at Fair Park, an all-black coed public school on the other side of town. The ladies of SVA were typically the daughters of Shreveport's elite: doctors, lawyers, business owners, and other professionals. Ingrid's parents were both educators. Seamus was a professor of history at Centenary College and Kathleen was a math teacher at Agnew Town & Country Day School. Sixth-grader Moira was one of her pupils.

The world view they had developed from years of extensive travels and experiences was often at odds with both the provincial nature of Shreveport and the curriculum at St. Vincent's. Still, the school was the best place for a teenage daughter to be with its college preparatory experience. It did not have a track team for Ingrid like nearby Byrd High School, but it had a better academic reputation and a connection to the diocese that secular institutions did not. Catholic kids in Shreveport went to Jesuit and St. Vincent's and that was that.

For her first two years of high school, Ingrid had developed a reputation within the faculty ranks as a brilliant student. Her grades were outstanding, so too her classroom demeanor, and she excelled at delivering insights and profound thoughts through interpretations of problems that impressed her teachers. Ingrid, like her parents, had a thirst for knowledge and experiences. She rarely settled on the status quo answer; she always wanted a bit more information, as if it would be a small, internal victory to unlock another facet of a fact. To her classmates, Ingrid was the one with the right answers even though she was not extremely forthcoming in presenting those answers. She was often embarrassed that she knew them and no one else did. She had a streak of independence and expected the same from others, but still felt timid at times. She abhorred cheating and felt it an insult to the process of learning on one's own. Ingrid would never tell on anyone who was cheating, but she certainly would not engage in the practice herself.

When people thought of her, it was as the smart girl who had a little bit of a fire inside of her soul that had not yet shown itself. She was not a pushover. She was silently strong and she was going places and no one in Shreveport, or anywhere else, was going to hold her back. Still, like most teenagers, she was also a mass of contradictions.

CHAPTER TWO

Though mature intellectually, Ingrid was a tad naive socially. Her first and only kiss was on the front porch of her house after a holiday dance at Jesuit's gym. It lasted as long as it took for her father to immediately rise from the couch after hearing footsteps on the front yard's gravel walkway, stroll to the door, and flip the switch of the porch light off and on again. Boys in high school did not seem to be interested in her. The only looks she got were from the married men she passed on her morning runs. She felt their eyes upon her legs, the ones striding by and glistening as the sun rose over the Red River in the distance. It seemed like every girl at St. Vincent's had a boyfriend who played football at Jesuit, or was in a rock band at Captain Shreve High School, or was a cowboy from Southwood High School. Ingrid would go to dances with her friends and to athletic events, but she and Laura were not the ones who got approached. They were not the ones being felt up in the backseat of cars parked out in the country, or the ones being kissed and ground upon in darkened living rooms.

The same could not be said for the two rival groups in Ingrid's class. Both were made up of three girls whose tendencies for glamour were surpassed only by their willingness to do anything for attention. All six had been friends in elementary school, but there had been a falling out over something as serious as the same dress being worn to the same birthday party and that calamitous event had severed the union. Three—Becky, Sarah, and Danielle—

evolved to become preppy brats with too much lip gloss and too much spending money. Their rivals—Cami, Carole, and Meredith—became the rebels who drank beer, smoked cigarettes, and generally became an affront to the social sensibilities of the other three.

It was, presumably, a high school dynamic not unique to history. For SVA, though, it was like a resumption of the Civil War. These six girls were in the limelight and everyone else had to select a side. Most went with what was referred to as Team BSD. That was the safe pick. Becky and Sarah's fathers were on the board of directors for St. Vincent's; Danielle's dad was the district attorney for Shreveport.

Few people chose Team CCM. These were the girls who ditched class to go waterskiing at Lake Bistineau with college guys. They were constantly in detention for having skirts too high and blouses unbuttoned too low. Cami smelled like unfiltered Marlboro cigarettes; Carole and Meredith emulated the mods of *Quadrophenia* by wearing trench coats with rock band patches and all three were as likely to beat up boys as they were to drag race a police car. Team BSD raised its collective noses at Team CCM, a quite ironic situation since all of the girls lived within blocks of one another in their neighborhood of Spring Lake. Louisiana still offered driving licenses to fifteen year olds in 1981, so having these rival groups racing each other up and down the famed *Thrill Hill* of Gilbert Street was not something for the faint of heart. Ingrid and Laura never really took sides with either group. Instead, they observed the fighting and the fray of the cliques from a distance and mocked the sycophants who aligned with one or the other.

Oddly, the two factions ruled the school even though they were just sophomores. The older girls had tried to keep them in check and discipline them, but that was impossible after an incident in SVA's courtyard earlier in the school year. During lunch period, Becky Harken had been challenged by a senior about her interest in a particular Jesuit boy. Instead of backing down, Becky slapped her rival across the face. Twice. The entire school seemed present to witness the moment. The senior girl retreated in a weepy huff and Team BSD celebrated its victory.

"Let that be a lesson to all of you bitches!" screamed Danielle.

The other girls at the school took notice. So, too, did Cami, Carole, and Meredith. A mutual respect seemed to exist between the two teams despite the fact that they were bitter rivals. The word *bitch*, of course, was the most common exchange for the factions. Passing each other in the hallways of the school always drew a nearly inaudible "Bitch" from under their breaths. "I hate that bitch!" and "What a bitch!" were usually the phrases exclaimed when one clique was talking about the other. After less than two years at St. Vincent's, Team BSD and Team CCM had alienated all of the older students to the point of surrender and dominated their fellow sophomores and the ninth grade class to the point of slavery. Ingrid and Laura, however, were exempt from these classifications.

Laura lived alone with her mother, the widow of an Air Force pilot who was killed in a B-52 crash shortly after takeoff from Barksdale Air Force base in Bossier City just across the river from Shreveport. Like Ingrid, she was studious and sincere, but she also had a combative streak that often clashed with the two popular cliques. Laura, like a lot of military brats, felt a bit of a chip on her shoulder because of a perceived social exclusion by local elites. Laura saw herself as an underdog and, thus, became a champion for the underdogs at St. Vincent's.

While Ingrid was more measured in her responses to injustices, Laura blurted out her feelings and was fearless in the face of potential discipline from teachers and administrators. Their friendship had an excellent balance with their roles as agitator and peacemaker. Together, they not-so-silently represented the interests of the girls who did not fall into line behind one of the two teams. Ingrid and Laura simply ignored the ruling cliques and, in doing so, gained the respect of their peers.

It was the first week of May and summer break was just a few weeks away. There was a buzz in the air at school for all of the girls. Maybe it had something to do with the longer days, the sun on the skin, or the music blaring through open car windows on weekend nights. Driving around Shreveport was really the only thing to do for fun if one was not at a lake, or by a pool, or at Mall St. Vincent. Cami McMillan was fond of asking "How cool can it be to hang out at a mall that's a parking lot away from a school with the same name?"

No one really knew where Team CCM hung out on weekends and few dared to ask. The assumption was that they were partying with older boys of dubious reputations. Ingrid and Laura went to movies, played board games, completed jigsaw puzzles, and spent a lot of time baking cookies with Moira.

They did not go to the parking lot of Johnny's Pizza in the Shreve City area to watch drunk boys from Jesuit and Captain Shreve get into fights that lasted less than ten seconds, nor did they scrape off the tops of frozen cherry drinks purchased at gas stations to add vodka, rum, or gin. Teenagers were bored in Shreveport during the school year when it was not football season. Friday and Saturday nights were spent cruising around looking for places to drink alcohol that were, with regularity, immediately discovered and broken up by concerned adults or the police department.

On Sundays, everyone seemed to disappear and Shreveport became a ghost town; people were either at church or at brunch or at home. Ingrid and Laura believed there was actually a huge conspiracy of which they were not a part with gatherings of people in huge tents outside of town for what they called Shreveport Meetings. Their imaginations would run wild because there was nothing else outside of their homes, activity-wise, to occupy their time other than sports they did not play.

CHAPTER THREE

Tuesday, May 5, seemed inconsequential like so many other days at the end of a school year. Still, there was much going on in Ingrid's world. Final exams were looming on the horizon, a lot of her friends at SVA were nervous because Jesuit's prom was approaching and they had not yet been asked, and Ingrid's mind was focused on her upcoming trip to Northern Ireland. She had, surprisingly, never been out of the United States other than some quick trips to Mexico when she was a baby. Her parents had traveled a lot before she was born, but with two children the family could not afford to take extensive international jaunts. There had been a road trip each summer to American landmarks like Yellowstone Park, the Grand Canyon, Yosemite, and Carlsbad Caverns. Piling into their station wagon had been a rite of passage for the Fallons: coolers held sandwiches and other snacks, the girls had the backseat piled high with toys and favorite blankets, and the tape deck was always playing classic Broadway musicals for family sing-alongs. Soon, Ingrid would be flying on a plane across the Atlantic Ocean to stay with relatives in Belfast more than 4,300 miles from Shreveport.

She had been a pen pal with her cousin there, Siobhan Fallon, for several years. There were photos of them together as infants, taken when her father's family had visited, but other than a yearly phone call on Christmas they had only corresponded through letters. Siobhan's father, Niall, was Seamus' brother and the plan was for her to stay with the West Belfast branch of the Fallon family for just over two months while volunteering part-time at St. Agnes' Parish. Faith was part of Ingrid's life and she was active at St. Joseph's Parish in Shreveport, though she vehemently objected to the fire and brimstone preaching of rabid Southerners at other churches. She enjoyed the sense of community, the outreach to the elderly and the ailing, and the feeling of satisfaction that she received from helping others. Her participation was such a counterbalance to the idiotic games of teenage life at school. What she did mattered more than matching the color of one's hair ribbons to one's eye shadow. Ingrid was not obsessed with the trappings of fashion and style. She enjoyed dressing well, like anyone else, and was presentable without trying too hard. Her quiet confidence unwittingly made her a campus leader.

The school bell rang and all of the girls came to order in Mrs. Morton's third period literature and composition class. What made this assemblage so unique was that it was the only time at St. Vincent's when all six members of both clique teams were together in one class. Ingrid and Laura were in the class, too, along with two of the three black girls at the school. Perhaps the cliques noticed their full complement of rivals present, but no one else saw anything out of the ordinary. Ingrid and Laura sat next to one another in every class they shared.

Mrs. Morton was a legend at the school. She had seen two of her daughters graduate from SVA and her son was currently a junior at Jesuit. Tall, erudite, and attired throughout the seasons with scarves and tortoise shell reading glasses, she had an aura about her that inspired the majority of her students to express themselves through creative writing and literary interpretation in ways that the crusty nuns at the school would never permit. Her classes were not a free-for-all orgy of liberalism, but they did provide a balance for the exploration of differing viewpoints.

One could be a dissenter and a Catholic, Ingrid figured, and Mrs. Morton provided the pathway to this understanding. Often, when reciting a poem to her class, she would lift her chin to the heavens and her eyes would partially close as if she was delivered into some mellifluous rapture. Mrs. Morton could discipline errant behavior with a glare and then hug with a grandmother's warmth. She was ageless, too, for her energy level and vibrancy made her seem like she was in her twenties instead of her late forties. Laura, especially, was riveted by her.

Mrs. Morton began to read.

"*All year the flax-dam festered in the heart,*
Of the townland; green and heavy headed
Flax had rotted there, weighted down by huge sods.
Daily it sweltered in the punishing sun.
Bubbles gargled delicately, bluebottles
Wove a strong gauze of sound around the smell.
There were dragon-flies, spotted butterflies,
But best of all was the warm thick slobber
Of frogspawn that grew like clotted water..."

She stood before the class and took a deep breath.

"Seamus Heaney wrote this in 1966," she said.

Becky, Sarah, and Danielle continued attempts to surreptitiously smack their bubble gum. They were not the type of girls to be touched by poetry. Cami, Carole, and Meredith sat in the back row as they did in every classroom and stared at Mrs. Morton with their heads resting at acute angles in the palms of their left hands. They typically mocked the conventionality of their teachers, but not Mrs. Morton. Meredith was friends with her son, Arthur, and made it clear to her cohorts that they had to be on their relatively best behavior in this particular class. Ingrid had been on-point with every word of the poem. So, too, had Laura. The only sound in the room was the din of a window air conditioner unit. Mrs. Morton moved gracefully back to her desk and sat down.

"Celeste, please come here and give me a hand," said Mrs. Morton.

Celeste Wilson was one of the three black girls at SVA. She always sat in the front row of her classes. There was, Ingrid often thought, something impeccable and regal about her. Celeste's skin was a dark tone of sable and she had the facial features representative of the flavorful Louisiana mixture of African, Creole, Acadian, French, and Native American. In two years of school together, Ingrid and Laura had shared classes and projects with Celeste but had never seen her on a weekend. They were always rivals for the top marks in school and had split the freshman year awards evenly between them: Celeste taking history and speech, Laura earning those for science and math, while Ingrid was awarded ribbons for literature and French. There seemed to be an unspoken mutual respect and acceptance between the three of them, yet an insuperable distance as wide as the very ocean Ingrid would soon fly over remained in place. Boys of different ethnic backgrounds went to high schools together and shared locker rooms with their teammates. Even in Louisiana, the veil of racism was often lifted by the camaraderie of popping towels off each other's asses and comparing female conquests. Girls did not have that sort of access to one another in a relaxed environment, so they remained separate and unequal.

Mrs. Morton handed a stack of papers for the class to Celeste, who took them and moved to distribute the assignments to each student. Up one row and down the next as whispering between classmates increased, Celeste handed out the stapled sheets and smiled when she made eye contact with a familiar face. When she got to the back of the room, Cami winked and blew her a kiss. This was the shock value that Ms. McMillan brought to St. Vincent's. She was as likely to emerge from a midday bathroom visit with a tampon tucked behind her ear as she was to flash a boob at a male teacher when his back was turned. Celeste grinned. She knew that Cami's bark was much worse than her bite and, frankly, she felt a bit flattered by the acknowledgement.

Celeste began walking up another row to the front of the class and, in her brief reflection upon Cami's ploy, tripped over a book bag that was in the aisle. She fell, face first, into a heap on the floor. Mrs. Morton's assignment papers went flying. There was no time for students on either row to catch her. Most of the room gasped. Some stood. Mrs. Morton heard the noise and looked up from her desk. Two seats away, Becky Harken smirked and uttered something under her breath.

"Dumb black bitch."

The sentence was loud enough to draw chuckles from Danielle and Sarah. A few others, mouths agape, sat stunned waiting for Celeste's reaction. Team CCM rose up in their chairs at the same time with looks of shock upon their faces. Laura was irate, yet frozen. Ingrid watched Celeste's every move. Mrs. Morton peered over the top rim of her glasses to investigate the commotion.

Celeste picked herself up and straightened her posture. She seemed taller than she was before. Ingrid looked at her compassionately, not sure what to do or how to reconcile her sympathy for the victim with her anger for Becky. Next to her, Laura was fuming. Her eyes were boiling and her fists were clenched. But, she was unable to move or speak. Celeste took a few steps and stood over Becky with an expressionless face. The entire class was captivated and expected a push, or a punch, or a slap. Everyone seemed to lean closer. with anticipation. Cami, Carole, and Meredith were focused and staring at the scene like snipers at distant targets. After all, the enemy of their enemy was their friend.

"What?" offered Becky, incredulously.

Celeste turned away and, as she did, made eye contact with Ingrid. It was a look that burned a hole into the soul, one that said *You can stop this* or *You can do something about this*. But, Ingrid had done nothing. Neither had Laura. Celeste passed out the rest of the assignment sheets and returned to her seat. Mrs. Morton asked if everyone was okay and the poetry lesson resumed. Minutes later, the bell rang and the girls went to their next classes. In the hallway, Laura grabbed Ingrid by the arm and they galloped into the restroom together.

"Do you believe that?" Laura shrieked. "Do you believe that just happened?"

Ingrid gazed through the bathroom's opaque window at the shadowy figures in the school courtyard. She wondered how fast word of this incident would travel and what the repercussions would be. She was also surprised by Laura's inaction.

"I cannot believe Becky would say that," Ingrid said. "She is such a pig. All of that money and privilege and she treats people like that. It's disgusting."

Laura nodded in agreement. This was an injustice. It was bullying. It was unsavory and unfair and blatantly racist. Becky's words were the antithesis of the Catholic education they were supposed to be receiving.

"What are we going to do about it?" asked Laura.

Ingrid looked into the eyes of her best friend.

"Do you think we should talk to Celeste?" she said.

Laura shrugged. She felt like confronting Becky, but what would that achieve? Would it start a war that involved all of their friends? Would it strain whatever semblance of positive relations there were with the three black girls at St. Vincent's? Ingrid usually had the more mature, less hasty perspective in these situations.

“I think we should wait and see what happens,” said Ingrid.

And with that, the day at school soon ended. Ingrid and Laura had not been gifted brand new cars on their fifteenth birthdays like many girls attending St. Vincent’s, so they usually walked home together. Their stroll took less than fifteen minutes. Laura lived just one block over from Erie on Delaware Street, making study sessions and sleepover parties all the more convenient. Today’s walk was different, though, after the incident in Mrs. Morton’s class. They both seemed to regret their inaction, yet did not know how to articulate that fact. Perhaps they were embarrassed. Perhaps they saw themselves as just immature teenagers unable to make a difference in a city like Shreveport that had always been segregated and ingrained with racial prejudice. Maybe they were too young and too inexperienced to know how to deal with the Becky Harken types on the planet. They walked into Laura’s house and poured some lemonade into ice-filled plastic tumblers.

“How do you think Celeste feels?” asked Laura. “Should we call her?”

“I don’t have even have her number,” Ingrid replied. “We’ll have to get it out of the directory.”

A horn honked several times outside of Laura’s house. The girls ran to the front window of the living room to see what was happening. It was Ingrid’s mother. Moira was in the back seat, asleep. The honk was the routine signal for Ingrid to return home, but the girls still ran to the window each day in the hope that it might be coming from a carful of friends or Jesuit boys. She grabbed her book bag and scrambled to the car, yelling “I’ll see you in the morning!” over her shoulder to Laura.

Back in her room, Ingrid collapsed onto the bed and stared at the revolutions of the ceiling fan. The collages on her walls of glossy photos from travel magazines blended with the posters of The Beatles, The Who, and The Rolling

Stones. She still had her impressive collection of ribbons from elementary and middle school field day competitions hanging from dresser nobs, too. Her mother had placed a family photo that was taken on her uncle's property near Cross Lake next to her vanity mirror, but Ingrid did not like to look at it. She felt ugly in that picture. Her memory of that time was ugly, too.

She thought of Celeste and the atrocity that she endured from Becky. *Dumb black bitch* rang in her head. She had heard it. Why had she not risen to her feet and slammed her fists down on her desk in a rage? Why had she not attacked the bully with a flurry of retorts? She thought about Laura's inaction. She thought about Celeste's reaction. Was it even a reaction? It was all so confusing. In one realm of her mind, her focus was on finishing the school year with excellent grades and heading to Northern Ireland. In the other was her fear that some girls at her school could get away with anything they wanted, whenever they wanted.

CHAPTER FOUR

Ingrid's sixteenth birthday, July 26, would be celebrated when she was staying with her relatives in Belfast. Sadly, that city was not in a festive mood in the first week of May nor would it be throughout the duration of her visit. On an island that was both an ocean and a world away from her troubles in Shreveport at her high school, tens of thousands of people were mourning. The news would not arrive to the Fallon's kitchen table until the following day but, when it did, Ingrid's life would be changed forever. She had always been a mild-mannered, good-natured sort who saw the best in people that she trusted. No one thought that any evils of the planet had ever visited her. But, they had. Ingrid kept them a secret as she blithely meandered through her existence as a good daughter, a good sister, and a good student. It was as if she had put blinders on herself to limit her own vision and to restrict others from seeing the pain in her eyes. Her daily smiles were an excellent masquerade for family and friends to digest.

Ingrid went to the record player atop a dresser in her room, turned it on, then moved the needle to the fourth song on the first side of U2's album, *Boy*. She mouthed lead singer Bono's words.

Into the heart, of a child
I stay awhile, but I can't go there
Into the heart, of a child

I can smile, I can't go there.

She could hear the unmistakable sound of Moira dragging toys while running up and down the wooden stairwell of their house. She could smell the aroma of her mother's stew that had been simmering in a crock-pot throughout the day. Ingrid reached down, touched her breasts, and wondered if they would grow as big as some of the older girls in her school. Hours of homework were ahead and the warmth of the afternoon sun on her hair made her feel comfortable. Despite her secret, Ingrid Fallon was seemingly at ease with herself and with her life. Her room was a safe haven. She got up from her bed and emptied her books, folders, and notebooks onto the floor. The next song on the album began to play. Its title was *Out of Control.*

The morning routine at the Fallon residence during the school year was probably typical for any family in America with two daughters and a home with one and a half bathrooms. There was a frenetic pace even with the therapeutic smells of buttered toast and coffee emanating from the kitchen. Ingrid and Moira always seemed to be ten minutes later than their mother would have liked; they shared toothpaste, makeup, and a mirror while singing show tunes aloud and harmonizing together. Ingrid would always do the finishing touches on Moira's bows, tying them to ensure they lasted the day. Moira would always give Ingrid a nod. It was the sort of gesture that said she looked good enough for any boy at Jesuit to admire.

Seamus Fallon would sit at his spot at the kitchen table with a pile of newspapers and magazines atop an extra chair nearby. He and Kathleen took the initiative to give their daughters an objective view of the world through as many possible sources that they could acquire. The girls, in turn, knew that they could not just go through the motions of stuffing scrambled eggs and home fries down their own throats at any family meal. No matter the hour. It was a ritual that was repeated five mornings a week: Ingrid and Moira would hop down the stairs, take their seats, and await the ideas of the day from their parents. The breakfast room allowed the rising sun to burst in unfettered and, often, the girls would have to squint a bit to see their father. He always sat with his back to the sun and cast a shadow upon them. Such was his radiance. Kathleen usually ate standing up at the kitchen counter, too busy organizing everyone's breakfast and lunches and getting a head start for the evening meal. She interjected from her perch, though, with witty barbs and the occasional off-color pun that always received a devilish smirk from Seamus.

They had a nurturing partnership. They were too smart and logical to be burdened with the fighting of younger, passionate couples. They were too intrigued with a continual thirsts for knowledge to ever become complacent and bored. They had traveled extensively together and had been exposed to many adventures and challenges. Most importantly, they had seen the challenges of others. The wisdom they imparted to their daughters was as much about true knowledge of historical facts as it was in the importance of objective interpretation of those same facts. That's what made living in Shreveport so difficult at times. Professionally, they were doing well. Socially, they had a network of friends and acquaintances through the college and the school affiliations of their daughters, plus through the parish. But, relative to the political climate and prevailing race relations, they were outsiders and idealists unwilling to succumb to the antebellum status quo. Seamus and Kathleen were going to inspire Ingrid and Moira to understand the world. They may not be able to change it, but they could teach them to change the world within themselves.

The Wednesday morning of May 6 was different. The girls noticed it when they bounded into the kitchen to eat breakfast. Seamus was sullen and brooding, like a boy who just found out that his bike had been stolen from the back yard. He was shaking his head in disgust at every page turn of his newspaper. Moira thought she had done something wrong. Ingrid seemed to sense that her father was extremely sad. Kathleen went to the girls and hugged them.

"A hero died yesterday." she said.

"Who?" said Ingrid.

"Bobby Sands," answered Kathleen. "He died on a hunger strike."

Both girls looked at their father and he managed a smile. It was his charm that made him so lovable, but he was not able to maintain the grin for long. Moira went to her father and kissed his cheek.

"I'm sorry, Daddy," she said. "I love you."

"I love you, too," said Seamus, his eyes glazed with the thin mist of a man showing emotions but unwilling to shed a tear down his face in front of his family at the kitchen table.

Ingrid and Moira took their seats as Seamus read from the papers. They heard names like Francis Hughes and Raymond McCreesh, places like HM Prison Maze and Long Kesh, and terms like special category, internment, and demands. It seemed so far away, yet they had family in Northern Ireland. Close family. Ingrid would be there soon. It was difficult for her to process the staggering load of information that her dad seemed to be regurgitating from the newspaper articles. Ingrid thought of how painful it must be to die on a hunger strike; she could barely go a few hours without eating. Her mother used to joke that she must have a tapeworm inside of her belly. She heard her father say that Bobby Sands died after being on his hunger strike for 66 days. She tried to think what she was doing 66 days ago and could not remember. She could not remember what she was doing 66 minutes ago, either.

Laura walked into the kitchen, grabbed a piece of wheat toast that already had butter melted on it, and plunked down her book bag as she sat at the table. Kathleen and Seamus considered Laura to be their third daughter and they certainly could never pick a better best friend for Ingrid.

"Who died?" asked Laura.

Fair question. The room had a pall to which she was quite unaccustomed in the Fallon home. Her liveliness and perky nature had not yet been contained by any sense of mature decorum, but that was to be expected. Kathleen brought over a cup of tea with milk and honey and placed her hand on Laura's shoulder.

"A brave man died in a prison hospital in Northern Ireland," Kathleen told Laura. "He starved himself to death for a cause."

Laura chomped down into her toast and took a sip of tea.

"That's sad," she said, speaking with a mouthful of food.

Seamus stood and left the table, steam from his coffee still rising from the mug. He had no appetite for breakfast or anything else. Kathleen followed him and the three girls were left alone at the table. Laura, always mischievous, pretended she was going to pull out one of Moira's bows.

Ingrid and Laura spent the day at school a bit more reflective than their classmates. They spent the remainder of the week that way, too. It was as if they had a secret about what was really going on in the world that no one else knew, yet one that they did not exactly feel comfortable bragging about to others. How would they introduce this knowledge? Who would understand it? On the heels of Becky Harken calling Celeste Wilson a *dumb black bitch*, they began to question how these evils could be combatted.

On their walk home together after school on Friday, Ingrid finally opened up to Laura.

"Is there anything you would die for?" she asked.

"You mean, like, my family and stuff like that?" replied Laura.

"Yes, that." Ingrid answered. "But also something bigger, like an idea. A cause."

"This thing with Celeste and Becky is really on your mind, isn't it?" asked Laura.

"Of course it is," Ingrid answered. "It's like we can't make up our mind about things that are important in Shreveport without understanding what goes on in the rest of the world. Like we need to look from the outside in and not just from the inside out."

"I wish I was going to Ireland with you," said Laura.

"I'm going to Northern Ireland," said Ingrid. "It's not the same country. Not at all, according to my dad."

The girls heard a horn honk several times and a car packed with horny Jesuit boys yelled out some gross utterances. Ingrid and Laura rolled their eyes and kept walking. They did not even offer some accepting smiles for the attention. It is not that they were disgusted, either, it was that they knew there was nothing to it. This was no flirtation. These boys did not want them. They were just targets of opportunity. Another weekend of making popcorn, watching movies, completing jigsaw puzzles, and listening to records awaited. Ingrid was looking forward to her run with her dad on Saturday morning. It would be a good way to relax in anticipation of the upcoming final exams that were already making her nervous.

The specter of the incident with Becky and Celeste at SVA remained in the back of Ingrid's mind, though, and it was coupled with the fact that her family would be visiting her uncle over the weekend. She had a difficult time putting it all together. On the verge of her life's first true adventure, Ingrid felt saddled with tinges of guilt and shame for not speaking up for Celeste in class. She had not made a conciliatory phone call to Celeste, either, and now figured that too much time had passed for it to make an impact or difference. Ingrid wanted to spend this particular Friday night alone. She did not want to hang out with Laura and she did not want to play board games with Moira. She wanted to be in her room listening to music and relaxing.

CHAPTER FIVE

The thought of wasting a perfectly good Saturday by going to her uncle's property near the lake for a barbecue disgusted Ingrid. He disgusted her. It was her father's other brother, Clooney Fallon, and it bothered her that most people in Shreveport called him Cloon. That nickname was too cute for him. Ingrid felt that it masked who he really was by giving him an appealing and friendly image. She could never remember if he was ten years older than her father or ten years younger. She did not care. His house on the family property by Cross Lake was a dump. It had a dock for a houseboat that looked like it would sink at any moment. There was an unfinished brick wall that ran about a third of the way from the street to the garage. It had been one of those ambitious, yet eventually unfinished projects like so many others at the lake house that her uncle had started. Ingrid had no idea what Clooney did for a living; he never seemed to do anything but smoke stale cigars, complain about politics, drink cans of beer, and watch sports on television. It was difficult for her to believe that he was a blood relative and brother to her gracious, loving, civilized father.

Seamus and Kathleen Fallon only knew the comical Cloon, not the putrid Clooney that Ingrid had experienced in the past. He was more of a running joke with them, someone not to be taken too seriously but serviceable enough to barely maintain the property. Not for Ingrid. For her, Clooney was a horrible babysitter. One time, Moira ran off at nearby Betty Virginia Park while he slept on a blanket and she was not found for several hours. Fortunately, she had decided to go to a friend's house nearby because her uncle was so boring. Moira was safe, but Ingrid never felt safe around Clooney Fallon. She had other bad experiences with him that she could not forget or tell anyone else about. So, each time she sat in the backseat of her family's station wagon for the drive to Cross Lake, Ingrid would feel stress in her neck and back that was bad enough to give her a headache. This Saturday's ride would be no exception.

She was so introspective and guarded at times, like a moat as wide as an ocean had been constructed around her soul. No one noticed this at school or at home, but Ingrid noticed it. It was as if she was outside of her body watching a person who was different than the one that everyone else thought they knew. Ingrid felt so blessed at times, so shattered at others, but perhaps it was all just the process of surviving her teenage years. This is what she convinced herself of when she felt this way. She longed for her trip to Northern Ireland. She wanted it to start today. She wished her parents were dropping her off at the airport instead of going to the barbecue at Clooney's house.

But here they were again as a family approaching the lake house on a driveway that had piles of bricks next to an unfinished wall. It was going to be her last barbecue before going to Belfast, but she would rather have been just about anyplace else on the planet. Clooney came out to greet everyone and his armpits were already wet from sweat, so too his cheeks and forehead. Ingrid could smell the hamburgers on the grill and that gave her temporary solace as his arms reached around her with a hug. He always seemed to hold the embrace a bit too long. It bothered her. Moira ran down to the water and Ingrid followed her. They liked to sit on the dock and watch people water ski in the distance. Neither could remember the last time that the houseboat was used. Even from their place on the dock, the old vessel smelled like mildew and rust was noticeable. It was like everything at the lake house: old, faded, falling apart, and possibly beyond repair. Just like the inhabitant.

Clooney always spoke loudly, too, and that bothered Ingrid. He did not have a hearing problem as far as she knew, so maybe he just felt the need to broadcast his thoughts because no one was really listening. Ingrid believed that her mother always had a skeptical eye for Clooney, but that she had been won over by his humorous side years ago and that was the impression that remained fresh in her brain. It made all of his issues explainable and acceptable. Seamus was always there to protect and coddle Clooney: he had bailed him out of a lot of jams before and he probably would again. That is what family did for family. This was what made Ingrid's special secret all the more confusing. Family was supposed to help family, not hurt it.

There was another confusing matter for Ingrid to consider. It was something that she never quite understood. Clooney, though born in the Republic of Ireland's Kilkenny region, never returned to Ireland or Northern Ireland to visit family members. There were a lot of Fallons on the island: cousins, aunts, and assorted distant relatives. Ingrid's mother had a large family still in Greece and Italy, as well in parts of Northern Ireland, and had visited many times. Seamus had made several trips there over the years to see Niall, too. Clooney never seemed to leave Cross Lake other than for his visits to their home at Easter, Thanksgiving, and Christmas. His gifts were always a bit off at these times, too. The sizes were never correct for the clothes he selected and the books he chose for Moira and Ingrid had already been read years ago. In Ingrid's opinion, Uncle Clooney was a disaster.

Her headache departed and her smile returned on the drive back to their house. It was the only place she had ever lived in and she always prayed that it would be the only home her parents would ever possess. She knew the location of every creak in the wood floors, how to properly care for the lilies in the garden, and where the best hiding spots were to surprise Moira. It was not so much a home as it was another member of the Fallon family. It had grown on her. She knew the most comfortable spots on the living room couch on which to recline and read. She knew how to wiggle though the doggy door leading to the laundry room from outside whenever she forgot her house key. It was the place in which she danced around the living room as a young girl, skinned her knees for the first time on the sidewalk while drawing with colored chalk, and shared sentimental moments while hearing the childhood tales of her parents. Ingrid was already envisioning coming home from college to visit and getting the home-cooked meals that dining halls cannot provide. Clooney's house at the lake was like a haunted house compared to this paradise.

It was soon another boring Saturday night in Shreveport and Ingrid had no plans. She did not have a date planned with a boy and had not heard from Laura. Moira sat, legs crossed, in her doorway and thumbed through a dictionary. That was Moira's thing: she wanted to learn every word in the world. So, with greater and greater frequency, she would grab a dictionary and scan random pages for words that she had never heard before. Then, she would read them aloud with their definitions to anyone within earshot. No one minded, certainly not Ingrid, who was often pleasantly surprised by her sister's discoveries. This is what made the Fallon home so unique. There was always a lesson to be learned and always a question to be answered. Seamus and Kathleen had inspired this voracious appetite for mind development in their daughters. It was not forced. Rather, it was organic to the environment. There were no secrets. The four of them liberally shared information with one another. That is what made Ingrid so uncomfortable at times with keeping her secret about Uncle Clooney. Her parents had always been accessible and approachable. Ingrid felt that she was letting them down by not being totally forthcoming.

She went to bed early that night and went for a run by herself on Sunday morning. Her father had gone to the YMCA in downtown Shreveport to play badminton with friends, so she used her time alone to knock out a brisk four-mile workout. Ingrid thought about what Becky had said to Celeste as she extended her stride and her heart rate increased. She thought about going to see Siobhan and her other relatives in Belfast. She thought about preparing for final exams. Ingrid liked the way her body felt when she ran. It was a cleansing. She felt so much energy that it gave her chills. She felt invincible. Each street corner she turned seemed to inspire a faster pace like she was a sleek race car on a grand prix circuit. Just a few more weeks and she would be on a plane across the Atlantic Ocean. That is what consumed Ingrid, in such a pleasant way, and she could not help but imagine that she would be a different person when she returned to Shreveport. Perhaps more mature, she thought, and more of a young woman than a teenage girl.

Her introspection was interrupted by the honk of a horn. It was Laura! She was driving her mother's car and it was obvious that Mrs. Wheeler was not enthused by her daughter's momentary lapse of concentration. Ingrid laughed and waved. They were kindred spirits in so many ways. It was as if they had a sisterly bond with the same DNA that allowed them to share moments together and communicate without ever saying a word. As she continued on the final stretch of her run home, Ingrid wondered if this was special to just them or if this was something that all girls their ages shared. She wanted it to be unique and something that no one else would ever understand. That is the way Ingrid was about a lot of things in life. She had a quiet demeanor that, coupled with her ethereal nature, made her appear almost angelic. But, there was also passion smoldering within her soul that was impossible to extinguish. She was ardent. She thought things through. Ingrid Fallon was not one to be underestimated, which is why her guilt over failing to defend Celeste by ridiculing Becky loomed so heavy upon her heart. As she rounded the final turn onto Erie Street from Fairfield Avenue, Ingrid wondered if she would ever have the strength to act in moments like that in the future.

CHAPTER SIX

It was Monday, May 11. Mrs. Morton stood before her class and smiled. There were only two more weeks remaining in the school year and she felt that great strides had been made since early September when the majority of her students did not know the difference between Lord Byron and Lord Jim. Final exams were approaching and foremost on the minds of the students, but St. Vincent's Academy also required its pupils to complete assignments over the summer break. The members of Team BSD appeared more interested in applying copious layers of mascara than hearing about reading lists. Similarly, Team CCM was using first period on Monday morning as nap time to recover from the weekend's revelry. Mrs. Morton surveyed the room and began to speak.

"Ladies," she said. "We have something special planned for you this summer."

Mrs. Morton always used the inclusive we when addressing her classes to bridge the gap between her supervisory role and the girls. It was her way of expressing that she was once in their shoes.

"Instead of giving you a list of three or four books that you will never read, I'm going to give you a creative writing assignment. We'll call it First Fiction."

The class groaned mildly.

"How many of you," she continued, "have ever thought about writing a piece of fiction like the ones you have read throughout the year?"

Silence. No one bothered to even stir. Mrs. Morton's offer was rattling around the brains of the teenage girls. Some thought it would be easy and some others dreaded the prospect. Ingrid and Laura looked at one another and smiled. They both did enough reading on their own to know they would not be missing anything by not having additional books assigned. This was a superior alternative.

"Can't wait for a piece of pie at Strawn's," whispered Laura.

"Me too," answered Ingrid.

One of their cute traditions as friends was to spend Monday afternoons at the old diner on East Kings Highway across from Centenary College where Ingrid's father taught. They would walk from SVA to Strawn's, eat strawberry pie, ogle college boys who worked there, then meet Seamus for a ride home.

"I'm going to encourage all of you to be as creative as you would like to be," Mrs. Morton continued.

"No rules, no subject limitations. Free form expression," she said. "I want all of you to let go and get your juices flowing to be honest and uninhibited."

Cami burst out laughing.

"Juices, Mrs. Morton?" she said.

The rest of the class giggled. Many thought they knew the double entendre that Cami was referring to and those who did not pretended that they did.

Mrs. Morton grinned with one side of her mouth.

"Miss McMillan," she answered. "You always have such insightful commentary. I cannot wait to read your story from the summer! Let us hope and pray that it is fiction."

With that, Mrs. Morton gave an appreciative wink as the class laughed together. It was one of those moments that only occurs at the end of the school year when guards are down, pretenses disappear, and everyone is too excited about summer vacation to be burdened with formalities. Ingrid made eye contact with Celeste. They smiled at one another. There was a sense from the acknowledgment that they were all in this together. But, Ingrid wondered, were they? Their worlds were so different. Shreveport was a segregated city. White people lived next to other white people and black people lived next to other black people. Church attendance was differentiated along similar lines. This bothered Ingrid. She could never understand why a church would not be fully integrated. It made no sense to her. It bothered her more that she had never said anything about it to other people. These were questions about issues that were just not brought up in Louisiana, not because they were not good to ask about but because there did not seem to be any possible difference to be made by asking them.

Would white people suddenly rush to black churches and would black people suddenly do the same to white churches? Ingrid pondered this and then went back to thinking about the pie she would be enjoying after school with Laura. She felt a bit of melancholy that the school year was ending, too, and thought about what it would be like to return in August after her visit to Belfast. She was so excited about flying by herself from Shreveport to Atlanta, then from Atlanta to Dublin. Siobhan would be meeting her in Dublin and they were going to take a bus from there across the border into Northern Ireland and, eventually, to Belfast. Ingrid imagined what it would be like to volunteer at the parish in Belfast's Andersonstown neighborhood. She thought about the connection she would be making with her father's family there and about all of the adventures she might have. Here she was—a teenage girl from Shreveport—avoiding the summer pool scene at East Ridge Country Club and tennis camps at Pierremont Oaks in Spring Lake by going to the country of her ancestors. As far as she could tell, no one else at St. Vincent's was going much further than Camp Longhorn in Texas. That's where

Team BSD went each summer. Ingrid had no idea what Team CCM had planned. She did not want to know, either.

After the delicious slice of pie at Strawn's with Laura, the rest of her week was relatively mundane. Ingrid spent most of her free time making a thorough packing list with her mother, preparing for final exams the following week, and getting a few early morning runs in with her father. They had a route together that looped around South Highlands across Line Avenue and onto the grounds of the Norton Art Gallery. Seamus liked to push Ingrid on the home stretch, too, by challenging her with a final sprint. He would never let his daughter win. She had to earn her victories. Ingrid's favorite part of the workout was cutting across the Norton lawn and feeling the crush of pine needles under her feet. It was not exactly a forest, but it gave the impression of one amid the charm of the surrounding homes. Sometimes, Ingrid and her father would race in and out of the trees by the museum in a cat-and-mouse game to see who could get the best angle back onto the adjoining street. She loved these moments spending time alone with her father, doing something athletic, and feeling the freedom that the regimentation of her typical day at school did not ever seem to provide.

Ingrid's weekend before final exams was spent doing what most teenagers do: studying, cramming, and stressing. She did not want to yield her awards from the ninth grade to anyone else. Her rivals were always going to be Laura and Celeste, but this year a new challenger had emerged. It was Cami. And, to Ingrid, that was quite an interesting development. She always felt that Cami, the definitive leader of Team CCM just as Becky was for Team BSD, had it in her to shine as a student. Ingrid felt mature feeling this way about a contemporary. It was as though she had recognized a diamond in the rough before anyone else. Ingrid reasoned that Cami had bigger dreams and aspirations than graduating high school, getting her college degree, and settling down in her early twenties in Shreveport to get married and have three or four children. Like Ingrid, Cami wanted out. Northwest Louisiana was a fine place to visit, or for retirement, but it was not where Ingrid wanted to be for long. She felt that Cami had even more of a pressing urge to leave because of her independent streak. The town was not big enough for them. Boston, Philadelphia, or Chicago were in their futures. Though Shreveport would always be home, it would be a hometown and not where Ingrid and Cami would blossom.

This is what made the wait to go to Northern Ireland all the more excruciating. Ingrid knew almost nothing about daily life in Belfast and that is what made it so exciting for her. She thought about where she would run, how she would get to museums, and when she would see the docks where the Titanic was built. Her father and mother had given her a multitude of kitchen table briefings about relatives and family history, but soon she would get to live it. Ingrid wanted a firsthand account of Belfast just like the writers and photographers she admired in travel magazines. This was her first expedition, her first safari, and her first true chance for individuality. No one really knew her there, even her cousin Siobhan, so whatever identity she had in Shreveport and at SVA could be examined by objective eyes.

Ingrid was plagued, though, by one sad thought. She loved romantic movies, especially the classics, and she longed for a boyfriend to bid her farewell at the airport. She imagined writing letters to him each day and of a joyful, tearful reunion upon her return. Ingrid dreamed of the flower field scene when two young lovers sprint toward one another and embrace, seemingly never letting go. There were boys who drew her interest in Shreveport. She found a few to be cute, a few to be clever, but no one had shown an interest in her. She was not a slut. Ingrid did not need to give herself away to the clumsy hands of an over-zealous high school boy to gain social acceptance. That was for the team members, especially Becky, Sarah, and Danielle. On the occasions when there were school dances at Jesuit, she had gone with friends and that was fine with her. Still, when she was alone in her room listening to records from her collection, Ingrid would daydream about slow-dancing with a boyfriend that did not exist. She would think about standing on her toes to kiss the boy that she loved and of walking hand-in-hand at the mall on the way to a movie. Ingrid wondered if there were a lot of girls like herself out there in the world. She was intelligent, fit, and pretty. Maybe she was intimidating. Maybe she had earned a reputation as a good girl who would not put out. Maybe people thought she and Laura were lesbians because they spent so much time together. She just could not be sure. All she did know for certain was that she had never been in love and wanted to feel that sensation.

For Ingrid Fallon, that moment would come sooner than later.

CHAPTER SEVEN

Ingrid felt like an adult when she changed planes in Atlanta at the international terminal. She had her passport in her purse, plane tickets, and traveler's checks in a secure money belt hidden by her jeans. She wore black sunglasses that looked just like the ones worn by Audrey Hepburn in Breakfast at Tiffany's. Ingrid felt worldly and cosmopolitan even though she had yet to experience anything extraordinary. Making the journey from Shreveport to Belfast felt like going to the moon for her.

She settled into her window seat and soon caught a glimpse of the Atlantic Ocean. It would be her friend for the next third of a day. Ingrid thought about explorers from Europe traversing it in the opposite direction to discover the new world. She imagined conditions on those sailing ships hundreds of years ago compared to the comfort and ease of travel on a jumbo jet showing movies. Ingrid thought about what it would be like to be greeted by Siobhan at the airport. They looked so similar that they could be sisters and Ingrid was sure that is what many in Belfast might think until they heard her Louisiana accent. Ingrid did not have a pronounced drawl, but she spoke clearly and methodically with a lark-like Southern ease and charm. The larger and more difficult the pronunciation for others, the more her voice sounded harmonious. Years of trying to properly pronounce foreign cities on the map in her kitchen and being corrected by her parents had given her a confidence to grasp any word in the dictionary. She had taken great pride, as the older sister, in being able to correct Moira in their vocabulary exchanges. Ingrid thought about learning a few words and phrases in Irish Gaelic, too, and hoped someone in Belfast would be able to teach her.

She awoke to the voice of a flight attendant over the plane's speakers alerting passengers to prepare for landing. There was a declaration card for clearing customs that she needed help with, so she asked the elderly couple seated next to her for assistance. It was then that Ingrid realized she had hardly said a word to them the entire voyage other than an initial, cordial greeting. Lesson one, from this moment forward she promised herself, was to engage with as many people as possible to learn as much as she could. Her body may have needed the several hours of sleep, but she regretted losing the time that could have been spent chatting with the cute couple in the seats to her right.

Ingrid walked off of the plane and immediately breathed in the cool, moist air of Dublin. She had left the stifling humidity of Louisiana and Georgia just hours ago and now her arms were marked with goosebumps. Was it the excitement of the moment or the temperature? Ingrid felt her pace quicken as she walked the ramp into the terminal. She was in Ireland! All of the planning for the past several months—all of the preparations and all of the research—had been for this moment. Ingrid had landed in a foreign country by herself at the age of fifteen and she felt a sense of accomplishment. It was as if a curtain in front of a movie screen at Mall St. Vincent had opened and the film about to begin was about her. Ingrid was the star of her own drama. She was not dancing around her room with imaginary boyfriends or running on the same streets in Shreveport; everything she saw or did from this moment forward would be for the first time.

Through the clearing of the people in front of her, Ingrid spotted Siobhan with the most obnoxious welcome sign in Dublin's airport. "You're Here, Ingrid!" was written on a neon yellow poster board with green glitter. It was unmistakable and, to Ingrid, it was gorgeous. She ran to Siobhan and they hugged, laughing loudly to erase any feelings of doubt or discomfort. Cousins and longtime pen pals had been united, finally, in person. Glitter from the sign sprinkled upon their blouses and onto the ground. They were giddy together. A grand adventure for both was about to begin and Siobhan was going to be the tour guide.

"You made it," Siobhan yelled. "You finally made it here!"

"I'm so excited," Ingrid answered. "This is the best day of my life!"

They hugged again and turned to walk arm-in-arm to the baggage claim area. Siobhan had planned everything to perfection with military-style perfection. She had been to Dublin many times and was a veteran of border crossings in each direction. The girls would catch a bus at the airport, take the M1 Motorway to the border of Northern Ireland just south of Newry, then connect onto the A1 through Bainbridge and Lisburn until they arrived in Belfast. The bus trip would take about three hours, according to Siobhan, and though Ingrid really wanted the chance to sightsee around Dublin, she could not contain her excitement about getting to see her aunt, uncle, and other cousins.

Niall was her father's other brother. In Ingrid's opinion, though they had never met in person, he was definitely the good one compared to Clooney. Her aunt was named Mary and she had two male cousins other than Siobhan. Cullan was thirteen and Ciaran was seventeen. Ingrid could not wait to meet all of them. She was teeming with excitement. It was mid-morning by the time Siobhan and her boarded the bus and, though she was feeling a bit fatigued, the nap on the plane had done its job for Ingrid. Her head was on a swivel. She was fascinated by everything she saw and that included road signs and billboards. One of her goals for the summer had been to keep a journal and use that as the basis for Mrs. Morton's writing assignment, so she furiously scribbled notes as Siobhan provided commentary. Her first fiction could be historical fiction.

Soon, the bus was in the lush Irish countryside north of Dublin and the girls settled down. Ingrid asked about Siobhan's house, neighborhood, and friends in the Lower Falls area of West Belfast. She inquired about breakfast and dinner times. She wanted to know about the parish and, since Siobhan would also be volunteering there, what the other people were like. They laughed and giggled and snorted aloud. The two were peas in a pod, thick as thieves, and wrapped in their own world of being cousins. It was almost like they were looking into a mirror when speaking to one another. Same age, same facial expressions, and the same mannerisms made them appear to be twins. This was soon noticed by a young man seated behind them.

"The two of you sisters?" he asked.

Ingrid and Siobhan wheeled around in their seats to see who was speaking to them, looked at one another, and continued with their giggles. They turned to face front again and each turned red as beets.

"I'd rather talk to your faces than to the back of your skulls," said the boy. "Where are you going today?"

"Belfast," answered Siobhan curtly. "And what business is it of yours?"

"My name's Declan," he answered. "What are yours, birds?"

"Do I look like a bird to you?" asked Siobhan. "You'll have to do better than that. We don't have wings."

"I'm Ingrid."

Her bravery came out of nowhere and Siobhan patted her cousin's leg in shock.

"Well, nice to meet you Ingrid," replied Declan. "You're not Irish."

"Irish-American," said Siobhan. "And, again, what's it to you? We're busy."

"Oh, I love American girls," said Declan. "So much kinder than Irish smart lasses. Get it?"

"I'm part Greek and Italian, too," offered Ingrid.

"That's a spicy combination," he answered. "I like that."

"Well, you look like you would like a bath and a haircut, too," piped Siobhan.

She was used to rogues on bus rides and wanted to protect Ingrid from this one's advances. The streets of West Belfast had taught her moxie. Declan had the look of a boy that mothers always warn their daughters about but are powerless to restrict them from in situations like this. His jeans were too tight and had too many holes, his leather jacket looked like it had been held underwater for months, and his hair was jet black and greasy. He wore black combat boots and his t-shirt may once have been white. HIs face was chiseled and his cheeks were rosy. The grin he possessed was a bit slanted, yet enticing to the girls in some manner that they could not describe, which made the pursuit of continued conversational engagement all the more devious. There was a noticeable scar above his right eye. Most people would take one look at Declan and not bother asking how it got there. Siobhan was not like most people.

"What happened to your face?" she asked Declan.

"Football accident," he replied. "Gaelic football, Miss America, not that game you play over there with all of the helmets and padding."

He was directing his words and his eyes to Ingrid. She could barely turn her head more than a few degrees in his direction without turning deep shades of fluorescent red. This was the first boy she had spoken to in Ireland and he already held some sort of captivating spell over her.

Something told her that Declan was trouble, but another voice inside of her head said to enjoy the moment.

"This is my cousin, Siobhan," said Ingrid. "She's my bodyguard."

"Lucky her," said Declan

"You won't be the lucky one, either," said Siobhan.

"I'm already lucky," he said. "I've met the two of you on this bus."

"Don't do us any favors, will ya?" said Siobhan.

The girls heard the unmistakable sound of a beer can being opened. Declan took a generous gulp and extended it between the gap in the seats for the girls to enjoy.

"If you think I would take a sip of that after your filthy mouth's been on it," said Siobhan. "Never!"

"My mouth is not that filthy," answered Declan. "I've only had seven cavities."

"I've never had a cavity," said Ingrid.

"Well, then, you haven't been eating properly," said Declan.

"You're gross," yelled Siobhan. "We can move to other seats, ya know."

"Go ahead," Declan replied. "More leg room for me."

With that, he slid down and threw his legs over the top of their seats. Ingrid could smell the polish on his boots. Siobhan took her hands and pushed Declan's feet back.

"Not today, sailor," she said.

"A boy's gotta try," said Declan.

With that, the interplay ended and several minute of uncomfortable silence ensued. Siobhan was accustomed to these exchanges of flirtation involving verbal sparring. Ingrid was not. For a moment, she felt sheltered and afraid that she did not know as much about teenage life as she thought she did. This was frustrating for her. Declan may have smelled poorly and displayed no care for traditional good taste, but he was showing interest and that is what she had enjoyed about the exchange. He was funny to Ingrid in a way that boys at home in Shreveport were not. Declan did not seem to be worried about what other people thought of him, at least not the two girls sitting nearby. Ingrid found that to be an attractive, strong quality in a boy. It was refreshing and made her feel alive.

CHAPTER EIGHT

The bus began to slow down and Ingrid looked out the window.

"The checkpoint," said Siobhan. "I bet you've never been through one before."

Ingrid nodded as she saw the Union Jack flag flying above a small building. There were soldiers everywhere. There were guns and vehicles everywhere. This was not like passing into California and having an officer ask if you had any fruits or vegetables in your car. They were entering Northern Ireland. She sensed motion behind her. Declan's boot kicked the back of her seat inadvertently. Ingrid turned around to look at him expecting an apology, but he did not notice her. His eyes were fixed on the British soldiers near the bus. He was no longer smiling. Declan looked scared. This was not the same boy that was chatting them up minutes ago. One of the soldiers came onto the bus and began walking down the aisle to the back where they were seated.

"This is routine," said Siobhan to Ingrid. "Nothing to worry about."

Upon first glance, Ingrid thought the soldier moved like a robot. Then she looked at his face. He could not have been more than a few years older than her. Another teenager, she figured, but with a uniform and machine gun. His eyes had deep, dark circles under them and his skin tone was pale. She became afraid and felt that the soldier was afraid at that moment, too.

He got to Declan's row behind them and stopped.

"What's your name?" said the soldier to Declan.

"Ronald Reagan," answered Declan.

Softly under her breath, audible only to Ingrid, Siobhan said "Stupid."

"Off the bus with me, now," said the soldier, emphatically. "We have a comedian here. Any more comedians?"

The soldier made direct eye contact with the girls and everyone else nearby on the bus. No one stirred. With both hands on his weapon, he directed Declan off of the bus. As they made their way up the aisle, the soldier jabbed the tip of his barrel into Declan's back.

"What's going to happen?" Ingrid asked Siobhan.

"I hope nothing," said Siobhan, suddenly less playful than minutes before.

So much was happening so quickly it was almost impossible for Ingrid to process any of it. She was on a bus ride with a cousin she hardly knew traveling through countries she had never visited before and now the one stranger she had encountered was being led away at gunpoint. Ingrid felt her hands begin to shake. A crowd of soldiers was now circling Declan outside the bus. They moved like alligators that jab and poke at prey before pouncing in for the kill. Declan, to his credit, was still smiling. Ingrid noticed this. He had his hands up and was replying to the soldiers, but she could not make out what he was saying. Everyone looked so young. Siobhan grabbed her hand and held it snug. The two girls had their faces to the window of the bus. So did the other passengers. Oddly, though, no one made a sound. Everyone was too frightened to breathe.

The first strike was the butt of a rifle to Declan's spine that crumpled him to his knees. The next was a kick to the ribs followed by a fist to the back of his head. A soldier picked up Declan and pushed him against the bus.

He was about five feet away from the girls when the flurry of punches and kicks rained upon him. There were at least eight soldiers involved in the brutal assault. Ingrid felt like she was going into shock. She could not scream and she could not cry. She just watched, helplessly, like when she had watched the aftermath of Becky calling Celeste a dumb black bitch.

Declan fell to the ground. He was a bloody mess. The soldiers had beaten him senseless. Siobhan and Ingrid watched as a man in a suit stepped forward from the background. He appeared to be the person in charge because the soldiers clearly deferred to whatever he was saying. The man stepped closer to Declan and gazed over him. Then, he kicked him in the head.

Siobhan let out a wail. Ingrid sobbed. Others on the bus turned their heads away. Two medics approached carrying a stretcher and Declan was hoisted upon it, but not before his wrists and ankles were shackled. The bus began to move north.

"Is this why Bobby Sands died on his hunger strike?" asked Ingrid.

"Yes," answered Siobhan. "And a lot more, too."

The cousins held hands so tightly that their knuckles turned white. Ingrid felt like she had gone from the gorgeous pastoral countryside of Ireland to a war zone in Northern Ireland. Was she in the Middle East where behavior like this seemed commonplace in the news, or was she in Europe? Had her parents been shielding her from the reality here? Ingrid thought back to her father's reaction when the news of Bobby Sands' death had reached their kitchen table. She remembered thinking about the physical torture of not eating for 66 days and wondered if it hurt as much as what Declan had just suffered. Ingrid did not even know his last name and he did not know hers. It had all happened so quickly, from the soldier boarding the bus to the beating, and she was devastated.

Suddenly, her elation at being there shifted to feelings of homesickness. Maybe lounging about Shreveport with a boring summer job and doing puzzles with Moira and Laura was better than a life of adventure abroad. She had to process this. She had to make sense of it. That was her nature. And, now, that nature had been affected by an event so catastrophic compared to any prior experiences in her life that she sat in stunned silence.

Siobhan began telling her stories of life in Belfast during the Troubles. This period began in the 1960s and was defined by the struggle of those on one side in Northern Ireland wanting unification with the Republic of Ireland and those loyal to rule by Great Britain. Ingrid had a difficult time listening intently and concentrating. It seemed like her cousin had an encyclopedic knowledge of history in the region. Siobhan spoke so fast and so much information was hurled Ingrid's way that the chatter became more or less background noise to the man snoring in the next row and the hum of the bus engine. She tried to imagine Declan showing up for classes at Jesuit High School dressed in his leather jacket. He could not have been more than seventeen, just like that solider on the bus with the machine gun could not have been more than nineteen.

An uneasy purr returned to the bus after about thirty minutes had passed. Passengers began speaking to one another again, but each conversation was in hushed tones. Ingrid and Siobhan stared out the window and tried to enjoy the passing views, but the impression of the beating they had witnessed would not leave their minds. The feelings swelling in their hearts were difficult to express and articulate. They were teenage girls, not mature adults, so the emotions of the moment were overwhelming in the relative context of their prior life experiences. Siobhan had thrust many acronyms at Ingrid. She needed a glossary.

PIRA. UVF. RUC. INLA.

It was all very confusing to her. This was Ingrid's first day in Ireland, first hour in Northern Ireland, and her first trip away from home by herself. The only acronym she had ever really cared about was SVA. She was here for humanitarian purposes—to volunteer at St. Agnes in Belfast—yet she had just witnessed the most inhumane treatment of another human being imaginable, at least, to her. Ingrid could not calculate what would come next. All she wanted, at this point of her journey, was to find solace at the home of Niall and Mary, to climb into a comfy bed, and to sleep forever.

It was Monday, May 25. Two months and a day from her sixteenth birthday. Ingrid felt so much older already. It may have been the fatigue of travel. It may have been the roller coaster of emotions from having a conversation with an intriguing character like Declan one moment to seeing him obliterated by British soldiers the next. She turned to her left to say something to Siobhan, but her cousin was sleeping. Under better circumstances, Ingrid would have snapped a photo of her for a laugh later. Siobhan's mouth was open, there was slobber dribbling down her chin, and she had a bug crawling atop her nose. This was not the time for humor, thought Ingrid. She would let Siobhan rest.

A few minutes later, Ingrid caught her first glimpse of Belfast in the distance. There seemed to be a grey glow above the buildings. Not smog, she thought, but not fog either. It was as if her current mood had been perfectly captured by the city to greet her arrival. This is the connective way that Ingrid thought. Her love for history gave her a sense of continuity in the world, from age to age, and she absorbed whatever surroundings she happened to be in with her own feelings. Ingrid was a chronicler of her own life with her notebooks and journals, but she also was a sponge for the decor of a memory. Friends in Shreveport marveled that she could always recall what people were wearing, or what someone said, or what rooms may have smelled like at a certain event. She was not a savant; instead, she developed her remarkable memory through the discipline of intense concentration. Her mother casually described Ingrid's prowess as taking it all in.

Now, approaching Belfast for the first time, Ingrid was at it again.

CHAPTER NINE

The bus jerked to a sudden halt with screeching brakes at the Europa Station on Great Victoria Street as Siobhan coughed and burped herself to consciousness. Ingrid, despite her level of fatigue, found a second wind in the bustle and speed of everything outside of her window. People seemed to be moving in fast-motion which, as anyone who has ever been there knows, rarely takes place in Shreveport. Checking first to ensure they had everything in their purses, the girls exited the bus and waited for the driver to pull Ingrid's suitcase from the storage area. The air was cool and crisp. It seemed much lighter than the humidity of Louisiana and it had a certain dissonance of scents. This was a city, not the tree-lined splendor of South Highlands, and Ingrid's sense of smell was teased with aromas of gasoline, exhaust, urine, beer, cigarette smoke, and fish frying at a nearby snack stand. The gritty nature of Belfast was foreign to her, yet attractive because of its differences to what she was accustomed.

That is the way she felt about Declan, too, and she could not seem to get him out of her mind. Nor could she be expected to after what had happened within just a few hours of her arrival onto the island.

"Siobhan! Ingrid!"

The girls turned their bodies in the direction of the passenger arrival platform to see Niall, Mary, and Cullan coming toward them at half sprints. Finally, Ingrid thought, she was actually here.

"An honor to welcome my beautiful niece," said Mary, gushing with joy and excitement.

"You look so much like your mother," added Niall. "We are so happy to have you! Has Siobhan told you a pack of lies about us?"

Ingrid, embracing the hugs and kisses from her relatives, grinned and shrugged.

"No, not yet," she said. "I'm hoping she gets it over with soon!"

Cullan played it cool in the background. At thirteen and the youngest of the brood, he was just coming into his identity and looked to be the typical teenage boy in Northern Ireland with sweatpants and a soccer jersey. He smiled at Ingrid and gave her a hug.

"I can't believe I'm actually in Belfast," said Ingrid. "I'm starving!"

"Didn't you feed the girl?" Mary asked Siobhan. "Ingrid, we know about your southern hospitality but we also have northern hospitality here!"

"Ah, ma," answered Siobhan.

"Sorry, Ingrid," said Niall. "You'll have to excuse our daughter. And you'll have to excuse our eldest boy, Ciaran. He's out and about and I guess meeting his cousin at the bus station was not on his list of things to do today."

"I look forward to seeing him," said Ingrid. "I look forward to seeing everything I can the next three months."

"There was trouble on the ride up at the border," said Siobhan. "It was awful."

"We'll talk about that later, girls," said Mary. "Now, let's get you both home and get some food in those bellies."

"I'm all for that," added Cullan.

His interaction drew a large smile from Niall, who put his arm around his son as they led the others to the family's car in the parking lot. Ingrid felt relaxed for the first time since she had left her bedroom on Sunday morning. Now, it was already Monday afternoon. She was very hungry and soon realized that she had not had anything to eat of substance since the airport in Atlanta. The flight to Ireland from there lasted almost nine hours and she had slept most of the way, so aside from a few pretzels and nuts while waiting in line to go through customs in Dublin she had not eaten a full meal.

On the car ride to Lower Falls, Ingrid felt like the roads and people moving about were even more frenetic than at the bus station. Niall drove south on Lisburn Road toward Belfast City Hospital and Queen's University, then made a right onto Donegall Road and another onto Broadway. Soon, they were at Falls Road.

"We're just a block away from dinner," Mary said to the three teenagers in the back seat of the family's silver Ford Granada.

"Can't wait!" answered Ingrid and Siobhan in stereo. They giggled at the harmony.

"Well, I might have to take a second job now to feed the troops," laughed Niall.

The car turned right onto Rockmount Street and Niall parked in front of the family home. All of the buildings seemed to be stuck together, Ingrid noticed, and she was not sure if her relatives lived in a house or an apartment. The neighborhood was, to her, old. It had history. It was a place without manicured lawns and flowerbeds, but it had a different kind of charm and certainly a lot of character. The green, white, and orange flag of Ireland seemed to be everywhere. Ingrid wondered whether she had arrived on some sort of memorial day or other holiday. She was too hungry and exhausted to ask any insightful questions, though, as she followed the Fallons into their home.

Mary kept a spotless and tidy house. There were porcelain figurines in display cabinets and the walls of the living room were decorated with family photographs. This was a typical terrace house and she recalled that her mother once explained the difference between a through house with its front and back door access and a back-to-back that is bricked on three sides. Ingrid saw many recognizable images on the walls. Her mother and father had a lot of the same photographs hanging in their own home. Now, Ingrid was able to begin the process of piecing together this distant group of Fallons with other relatives throughout the globe. First, of course, she had to eat.

Siobhan was in the kitchen helping her mother with the final preparations for an early afternoon dinner as Niall and Cullan led Ingrid to the room where she would be sleeping. It had recently been Ciaran's room, but he was in and out of the house so much that throwing a mattress down for him in Cullan's room seemed like the best option. Theirs was a three-story narrow home with three small bedrooms on the second floor and a master loft above it. Over the years, that loft had evolved to become Mary's room as Niall usually fell asleep, and stayed the night, on the couch in the living room. Mary enjoyed painting and crafts in her spare time; Niall, like his brother Seamus, was a history buff. He was also a music fanatic. Niall worked as a manager at an electronics factory near Belfast's docks.

Ingrid thanked Niall and Cullan for their help and started unpacking her suitcase. There was an empty, unfinished wood dresser for her to fill and a small closet in which to hang clothes. Like her room at home, there were posters on the walls of bands but only a few that she knew. Squeeze. The Sex Pistols. The Undertones. Ingrid was familiar with U2 and The Who, but the rest seemed pretty extreme to her. There were also posters of soccer players and teams, but she knew nothing about that. Ingrid wondered what Ciaran would be like. Cullan seemed normal. She adored Siobhan. Mary was going to be a fantastic aunt and host for the summer. And, in Niall, she saw a direct reflection of her father. As she continued to get comfortable in the room, a thought came to her that brought displeasure: why were her father and Niall one way and Clooney another?

Ingrid bounded down the stairs and into the kitchen. She had a high level of energy in this new environment, but the reality of being weary from overnight air travel was looming. Mary had a spread of food waiting: cold cuts, cheeses, breads, and vegetables to dip into sour cream. Siobhan was beaming. She felt like she finally had a sister in the house even though it was her cousin and pen pal. Cullan had run out to spend the afternoon with friends at the local athletic club's fields. Niall was already on his couch watching the news and reading a pile of newspapers. That looked familiar, Ingrid thought, and she let out a huge grin as another bite filled her mouth.

There was no sign of Ciaran and that was not surprising to anyone in the family. Ingrid was inquisitive about his absence.

"Will I ever get to meet my other cousin?" she asked.

"You'll meet him when he's ready to meet you," said Siobhan. "That's the way it works around here. Ciaran is on Ciaran's schedule."

"That's the truth," said Mary. "But he's a good boy. Wouldn't harm a flea."

"He has some cute friends," added Siobhan. "You'll meet a few when we go to the pub, Ingrid. I'll introduce you."

"The pub?" asked Ingrid. "The drinking age in Louisiana is eighteen."

"I thought it was twenty-one," said Niall, obviously listening intently from the adjoining room.

"Nope," answered Ingrid. "Still eighteen."

"Well, you don't have to worry about that here," said Siobhan.

Ingrid felt a rush of nervous excitement come over her. She had tasted wine, beer, and champagne on occasion, but to actually sit in a bar with adults and order a drink was beyond her scope. She thought of the times her parents had let her finish off half a glass of wine, but she also thought about the piles of crushed beer cans overflowing at the lake house. There had to be a happy medium.

There was much on Ingrid's mind. Her travel from Shreveport to Ireland, embracing Siobhan at the airport, seeing Declan beaten by the soldiers, arriving in Belfast, and now dining with her relatives. It was not so much overwhelming as it was surreal. How to explain it all? Mary got up from the table, went to the counter, and returned with an envelope.

"This came for you a few days ago," Mary said to Ingrid.

"What is it?" asked Ingrid.

"Open it!" yelled Siobhan.

Ingrid looked at the return address. It was from Moira. Her sister had used a green marker on the envelope and had drawn several shamrocks.

"This is adorable," said Ingrid.

She opened the letter and began to read it at the table. Her first impression was confirmed. Moira wished Ingrid good luck at St. Agnes and told her that she was going to miss her. She asked that Ingrid learn a lot about her family members so she could do skits about them when she returned. At the end, Moira told her that she would learn five new words a day until her sister got back to Shreveport. Maybe it was because of how tired she was or the drama of the day in general, but Ingrid burst into happy tears. Siobhan and Mary hugged her and Niall came over to pat her on the head. Cullan continued to stuff his face with dinner.

Ten minutes later, after brushing her teeth, Ingrid collapsed onto the bed in Ciaran's room. She was still wearing the clothes she had put on Sunday morning in Shreveport before her flight to Atlanta. With her face buried in the pillows and the lights out, this was Ingrid's first night on Rockmount Street in Lower Falls, West Belfast, Northern Ireland, United Kingdom. Ingrid was too tired to dream. Moira's letter was under her left forearm. A new world was hers to explore and experience. A new day was to dawn and, like her first one outside of the United States traveling by herself, it was one not to be forgotten.

CHAPTER TEN

It was Tuesday, May 26. Ingrid had slept through the night and woke up to the sound of young boys playing soccer in the street. She opened the curtains and looked down to see them running about and laughing on the concrete. Such innocence, she thought, and a remarkable contrast from the previous day. Ingrid felt refreshed and alive, even more so after she had showered and put on some clean clothes, and she was ready to start exploring Belfast with Siobhan. Their first stop would be St. Agnes' Parish, which was located less than two miles away in Andersonstown. That area was in the Upper Falls part of Belfast. Siobhan's family had lived near the parish for many years and, despite moving to Lower Falls, they still remained committed to Father McQuarters. The girls would ride bicycles to go to and from the church. Their route would take them past the historic Milltown Cemetery and Casement Park, home to a local hurling and Gaelic football club.

Siobhan led the way on their journey and Ingrid, though no stranger to running on the sidewalks of busy streets in Shreveport, felt a bit nervous riding a bike on Falls Road, through a roundabout—she had never seen one before—and on Andersonstown Road. She trusted her cousin, of course, and enjoyed the feeling of the crisp, dewy air on her face and through her hair. Ingrid had corresponded with Father Eamonn McQuarters for a few months, so she was extremely excited about meeting him in person for the first time. Siobhan had experience volunteering at the parish, so Ingrid felt that with her cousin's advice and Father McQuarters' guidance she would fit in comfortably in a short amount of time.

The girls carried their bikes up the front steps of the church and took them around the building to a courtyard in the back. Father McQuarters was already there watering potted flowers and smiled at their arrival.

"So, this is the American Fallon we've been anticipating," he said. "Welcome to St. Agnes!"

With that, he removed a gardening glove and extended his right hand while smiling at Ingrid. He seemed, to her, like the quintessential Irish priest she had seen in the movies. He was short, pudgy, had a cute button nose and white hair, wore thick glasses, and had rosy cheeks. His voice was calming and his brogue was thick. She had never seen a priest in work boots and gardening gloves before, so to see Father McQuarters with his shirt sleeves rolled up tending to lilies and roses was intriguing.

"Thank you," Ingrid answered. "I've been waiting for this a long time. Thank you for the opportunity. Siobhan has told me so much about St. Agnes that it's like I've already been here before."

"It will grow on you, my dear," he replied. "Siobhan has been a great help around here."

Father McQuarters turned to a beaming Siobhan.

"How's Ciaran been doing?" he asked.

"Never home, Father," said Siobhan. "We hardly ever see him. Always on the go. Always on the run, that one."

"Yes, yes," he said. "Teenage boys are nothing but trouble."

The girls giggled and started working on the flowers with Father McQuarters. As they did, he went through the expected responsibilities for the summer volunteer program. Siobhan and Ingrid would be preparing and delivering meals to elderly residents in the area. They would be working with young parishioners, similar to camp counselors, and producing musical numbers and scene performances. It would be like a summer day camp for the kids. When needed, they would work on assembling materials for mass services and help the choir with whatever was required. Ingrid was excited to help in the garden, too, because the lilies reminded her of home.

Father McQuarters gave them a tour of the church grounds and showed off a lot of the hiding places where children were known to disappear to avoid services and Sunday school. He seemed to have a demeanor unlike the clergy in Shreveport who often appeared to be overtly stern. Ingrid was so excited to be at St. Agnes that she kept stepping on the back of Siobhan's shoes; her eagerness was noticed by Father McQuarters, too, and he beamed with joy at the exuberance of the girls.

"Ten to four Monday through Friday and a little help on the weekends, please," he asked.

"Absolutely!" answered Ingrid.

"You don't plan on cutting into our social lives too much, do you Father?" said Siobhan.

"Oh, Miss Fallon" he said. "Your priorities will be respected!"

The girls left the church on their bikes and Siobhan led Ingrid on a quick tour of Andersonstown by her old house, then back to Lower Falls. The entire region was considered West Belfast. She wanted to give her cousin from Louisiana a real Irish pub experience, but first they had to lock up their bikes at home and have a bite of lunch with her mom. This was a part of the day that Siobhan always treasured. She grew up having the women outnumbered by the men, so the peaceful time with Mary Fallon allowed for the women to speak freely without being interrupted by Niall, Ciaran, and Cullan. Now, with Ingrid in residence, the odds would be evenly stacked.

Ingrid established herself on this first day as extremely helpful around the house. Mary and Siobhan were impressed at how easily she fit into the family. She was a blood relative and cousin, obviously, but she was also willing to be part of the crew. The three of them acted like they had been inseparable for years and Ingrid longed for as many moments like this during her visit as was possible. Maybe it had something to do with all of the stories her parents told her over the years about Northern Ireland, Ireland, Scotland, Wales, and England. She felt comfortable here because of her genes and her listening skills. Many nights nestled with Seamus and Kathleen being regaled with stories that had sunk deep into her soul made her sense that she had been here before, even though she had not.

"Ciaran and Cullan are playing football in the park," said Mary. "That's soccer to you, Ingrid."

"I know the distinction," laughed Ingrid.

"Your father was quite a good player in his day," said Mary. "He had a bit of pace."

"He's still a fast runner," said Ingrid. "We go for runs in Shreveport together. He doesn't let me beat him."

"You'll love the park, then," offered Siobhan. "It's not too far from my pub, too. Clancy's. It also happens to be just about at the end of our block to the left. You can go jogging and then have a few pints with me. I'll wait for you. Great jukebox there."

"It's been there eighty years," added Mary. "Lots of history for a history buff like you."

"Can't wait!" exclaimed Ingrid, who was curious about finally seeing Ciaran.

After lunch and some tidying up around the house, Siobhan led Ingrid to the corner of her street at Falls Road, made a left, and passed four streets until they were at Beechview Park. The luscious green turf was surrounded by thickets and sprinkled with trees. There seemed to be several collections of boys playing football, Gaelic football, and rugby. Siobhan waved and winked at a few familiar faces, then led Ingrid by the hand to a field area far to the left. She knew this spot as the one frequented by her brothers because, when they were kids, it had served as the spot to try stolen cigarettes and beer for the the first time. It held sentimental value. Siobhan pointed her brothers out to her cousin and, as they got within about twenty-five yards, something happened to Ingrid that would change her life forever. It was as if she had been hit by lightning.

She saw him. She gasped. She felt a lump in her throat. She felt nauseous. There was, for Ingrid, no similar feeling in her nearly sixteen years on the planet for comparison. At that moment, no two other people existed. Siobhan was rambling on about something right next to her but all she could hear was the frantic beating of her own heart as she watched him play soccer with her cousins and some other boys. His hair was dark brown, his skin fair, his eyes were hazel and he was a shirtless wonder to Ingrid. Sweating and moving with fluidity, he possessed the gaze of her eyes without even knowing it. The wiry muscles of his chest, stomach, and back seemed to tighten and contort with each change of direction and deft flick of the ball. There were eight or nine other boys playing, but they were invisible to her. She felt her legs go weak and put her hand upon Siobhan's shoulder for support.

"Who is the boy in the white shorts?" Ingrid asked.

"Tight white shorts, they are," answered Siobhan. "That's Padraig. Everyone calls him Paddy. Irish enough for you?"

"Is he nice?" responded Ingrid.

"They're all nice when they want you," said Siobhan. "It's after that when you have to worry. He's the strong and silent type."

"He's magnificent," swooned Ingrid.

It was an instant that is captured only once in a teenage girl's life, a split-second when she has unrecognizable yearnings for the first time that she cannot explain upon the sight of a boy so prepossessing she is moved to spasms. And that is what happened when Ingrid Fallon saw Padraig Fitzsimons playing soccer at Beechview Park with her cousins. She did not know how to define what was boiling within her and, for once, she did not care. To Ingrid, it was as if her veins had been filled with sunshine. She suddenly felt so warm and content yet, concurrently, also frightened by the hold the mere sight of a teenage boy with whom she had never shared a word or smile had upon her. Ingrid's dalliance of intrigue with Declan on the bus ride was erased and superseded. Padraig was the most beautiful person she had ever seen in her entire life and far better than any rock star or heartthrob hanging on her bedroom walls. This was the living, breathing personification of the imaginary boy she had always wanted to slow dance with in the gym, the one she wanted to sit by at the lake, and the one she hoped would throw rocks at her bedroom window late at night. Ingrid Fallon was in a glorious state of shock. It was love and lust at first sight.

CHAPTER ELEVEN

As Ingrid and Siobhan strolled several yards behind the group of boys on the way to Clancy's, Cullan tagged along with them. He was a few years younger than Ciaran and the rest, and he loved Siobhan more than anyone else in the world, but he was truly fascinated by his cousin from America. Ciaran ignored the girls. In fact, he had not even greeted them or invited them to the pub. Ingrid found that quite rude. It reminded her of Clooney. As she observed the strange new crowd in front of her, one thing became clear: Padraig was the leader of the group and the life of the party. She watched as he tussled the hair of one boy, pushed another, and lovingly mocked a third for some mishap on the field. There seemed to be a spirit to him. She wondered how all of this could be happening in just her second day away from home. Ingrid was riveted by Padraig's every move while, at the same time, trying to figure out the mysteriously quiet Ciaran.

Clancy's, according to Siobhan, had a fascinating history upon which she did not elaborate. Ingrid noticed the scarves for Glasgow Celtic FC hanging from the ceiling. Her father had one in their garage at home. It was his favorite soccer team and seeing the scarf in the pub made her feel comfortable. The boys went to a corner booth after ordering pints at the bar, while she joined Siobhan and Cullan at an adjacent table. One of the boys, a portly redhead named Jimmy, went to the jukebox and after a few moments *River Deep Mountain High* by Tina Turner was blasting from the speakers. Suddenly, the entire bar was singing along. Ingrid was fascinated. She could not imagine anyone in Shreveport spontaneously bursting into song with other people in a public setting. It was magical. Her head was spinning. She was in a West Belfast pub sitting within ten feet of Paddy Fitzsimons and one of her mom's favorite songs was playing. As well, she was sipping on a lager shandy. Siobhan had ordered the beer and lemonade concoction for her. Cullan opted for plain lemonade.

A series of old Motown songs played on the jukebox. Jimmy had made some pretty amazing selections, in Ingrid's opinion, and the patrons of the bar continued to sing along. The boys in the booth were loud, boisterous, and enjoying the afternoon after their battles at the park. Ciaran sat quietly next to Paddy. There was something about him that made Ingrid uneasy, as though he was not comfortable in his own skin or in social situations. All of these boys were his friends from the neighborhood, they were enjoying beers together in their pub, yet her cousin appeared to be out of place. It saddened Ingrid, but her mind and heart were so preoccupied with Paddy that she could think of practically nothing else at that moment. Jimmy got up from the table and greeted Siobhan.

"This your cousin? he said, pointing to Ingrid.

"Yes," answered Siobhan. "And don't get any ideas."

"I won't," said Jimmy. "I only have room for you."

"Ah, Jimmy," replied Siobhan. "Such a charmer."

"My name's Jimmy," he said to Ingrid. "What's yours?"

"I'm Ingrid," she replied. "This is my first time in a pub."

As soon as she had said those words, she felt awkward. Jimmy looked at Siobhan and laughed. Ingrid was mortified. She felt uncool again, or at least she felt that she had appeared uncool to Jimmy. Ingrid wondered how

Cami, Carole, and Meredith would be acting in this place. Would they be draped all over the soccer boys? Would they be flirting with the bartender? What songs would they play on the jukebox? Would they be singing out loud with everyone else? She was 4,000 miles from home and the desire to fit in with her classmates—the ones she thought cooler than herself—was heavy on her mind. She actually preferred Team CCM to Team BSD. Like the people sitting in Clancy's, they seemed real. They were not phony images of themselves like Becky, Sarah, and Danielle.

The door opened and, as it did, the song on the jukebox ended. Four men in dark blue jeans and black leather jackets wearing herringbone flat caps entered the bar. The boys looked up to notice them and, in the same motion, became quiet and looked down into their pint glasses. It was as if a record had scratched and everyone in the room froze. Cullan eyed them. Siobhan looked at Ingrid and took a furtive sip of her shandy. The men had stone faces and blue eyes. One walked with a slight limp. The bartender was already preparing their drinks as they took a corner booth in the bar's furthest end. All four sat facing the door. Jimmy did not get up to add more coins to the jukebox and Ingrid had no idea what was transpiring. An older couple hastily paid their bill and briskly exited. Ingrid could not stop staring at them.

"Stop looking," whispered Siobhan. "Don't let them catch you looking at them."

Ingrid was confused. She did not understand how the festive atmosphere at the bar had so quickly changed into something ominous. She looked to the table of boys and made eye contact with Paddy. He smiled. She looked away. When Ingrid looked back at him again, he was still smiling and looking at her. She froze, then tried to look sophisticated by taking a sip of her drink. In doing so, she spilled a mouthful down her chin and onto her shirt.

"Smooth," piped Siobhan. "That's a smooth move, my love."

The bartender delivered four pints to the men at the table. A few moments later, Ciaran and Paddy walked over to speak with them. Those left behind watched intently. Ingrid did, too, because her eyes were fixed on Paddy. Siobhan thought how disobedient Ciaran acted at home to their parents. In front of these four, he was like a sleeping puppy. Ciaran and Paddy were nodding their heads as one of the men extended a finger to point at them. Ingrid did not sense that the man was angry as much as we was instructional. Like many other aspects of her first two days in Belfast, she was confused. This was all new to her. These dynamics were foreign. She may have been able to understand the language, even most of the heavier Irish brogues like Father McQuarters had, but the interplay between people she had never met before—even her cousins and family—was something to be deciphered.

Ciaran and Paddy returned to their booth and sat down. None of their friends asked any questions about what just happened. Fergal, a tall boy who appeared to be uncoordinated in just about every motion of his body, stood up and started to make a toast.

"Here's to Jimmy," he sang. "Here's to Jimmy, he's a man of class. Here's to Jimmy, here's to Jimmy, here's to Jimmy he's a horse's ass!"

Normalcy and revelry returned to the table. The boys laughed, so did Cullan, Siobhan, and Ingrid. Paddy smiled at Ingrid and she smiled back. She kept thinking that she wanted to talk to him, but was not sure how an introduction would occur. Ingrid did not want everyone to see that she was interested in this one boy upon their first interaction. What had come over her? She did not know. She just felt it. He felt right. There was no pretense. There was no familiarity. Jimmy returned to the jukebox and soon the boys were singing again. A third or fourth pint will do that to a young man. Siobhan was on her second shandy, but Ingrid was still nursing her first. Cullan had finished off five or six lemonades.

The four men in leather jackets got up to leave the bar, but not before one went over to Ciaran and whispered something into his ear. After they had exited, Ingrid felt that the other people there had resumed breathing normally. It was like there had been a collective sigh of relief. She wondered who these men were. They did not look like those she was used to in Shreveport with khaki pants, golf shirts, and loafers. They did not look like the ones she passed on her morning runs. And, wisely, she made the decision not to ask Siobhan about them.

"When's dinner?" Cullan asked.

He knew that his mother always served dinner at 5:30 p.m. each evening, but his question was just a prompt for them to leave.

"You coming?" Siobhan yelled out to Ciaran.

"We'll be home soon," he answered. "Tell mom that Paddy is joining us."

With that, Ingrid felt panic. She tried not to blush, but the sensation of heat on her forehead and cheeks told her that she was most likely a shade of burgundy. She hoped that Paddy had not noticed. Walking out of the pub onto Falls Road, Ingrid felt like her feet were not even touching the ground. She felt as if she was being transported atop a cloud. Was it the one shandy? She had not even finished it. Siobhan held her hand and Cullan lagged a few steps behind as they made the right turn onto Rockmount Street. From meeting Father McQuarters at St. Agnes' Parish, to the special time with Mary and Siobhan, to watching the boys play soccer and discovering Paddy for the first time, to the bizarre scene at Clancy's, Ingrid felt inundated with sensory inputs. This was already so much better than being in Shreveport, she thought, and it was just her second day.

The trio entered the Fallon's home and went to the kitchen to help Mary with dinner. Ingrid slipped away to the bathroom for a moment, however, to tidy herself in anticipation of Paddy's visit. She loved saying that name in her head: Paddy. It fit him. Niall was fixing a broken lamp in the living room. Tools and parts were strewn about the floor atop a newspaper. He reminded Ingrid so much of her father. They were masters of all trades. She pulled Moira's letter out of her pocket and promised herself that she would send one letter a week to her parents and one to her sister. Ingrid thought about the weekly phone call she would be making on Sunday evenings, too. Her mother and father wanted her to have her freedom in Northern Ireland, but they also wanted regular contact. She was only 15.

Ingrid heard a commotion downstairs. Ciaran and Paddy had arrived. She checked her hair and face in the bathroom mirror once last time. No pimples. That was good. Nothing stuck between her teeth, either. She applied a quick spritz of perfume, turned to get a side view of herself, then smiled one last time close to the mirror for a final check. Ingrid could not remember a similar preparation before. Somehow, this first time came naturally.

An hour after dinner had finished, Ingrid could not remember what she had eaten. What she did remember was that she spent the entire meal staring at Paddy. He had barely uttered a word other than thanking Mary for the meal. Ciaran did most of the talking. He bragged about scoring the most goals on the field. He boasted about being able to drink more beer than his friends. Ingrid was nonplussed. Her cousin was obnoxious and weird. The two boys left soon after the plates were cleared and Ingrid went upstairs to bed. She could not stop thinking about Paddy and wondered if he had even noticed her. Just like in Shreveport, she felt invisible.

CHAPTER TWELVE

Three weeks passed before Ingrid saw Paddy again. That was an enormous chunk of her summer in Belfast without his presence. She had resigned herself to the fact that she would never see him again, too, until he showed up with Ciaran late one night while she and Siobhan were watching a movie. He smelled of alcohol and was obviously drunk. She thought of the dinner together with her relatives after the pub. Paddy had not said a word to her and she not a word to him. His only utterances were polite, abbreviated responses to Niall and Mary. Now, he sat himself down on the couch next to her like an old friend. It made her uncomfortable. Worse still was that Ciaran sat down on the other side. She felt suffocated.

"Do you mind?" blurted Siobhan, clearly upset about the interruption. "We never see you around here and when we do you ruin our evening."

"Shut up," said Ciaran. "Who asked for your opinion?"

"I will not be quiet!" yelled Siobhan.

Ingrid sensed a history of conflict between her cousins. It was as if the roof of the Fallon's home was not big enough for both of them and, with Ciaran's frequent absences, Siobhan had claimed the household as her own in the teenage hierarchy despite being two years years his junior.

"You'll do what I tell you," said an annoyed Ciaran. "You're a girl and girls listen to boys."

"Not in my world," answered Siobhan. "We'll get equality just like everyone else around here."

Ingrid felt Paddy's leg against hers. At that moment, the outside of her right thigh felt like it would spontaneously combust. She had settled into her routine with Siobhan at St. Agnes the past three weeks. They were teaching musical numbers to children, delivering meals to senior citizens, and helping Father McQuarters with parish operations. She had gone on several runs through the streets of Lower Falls, even into downtown Belfast by the shipyards, and was feeling a sense of autonomy. There had been nights at the pub singing songs and she had even been chatted up by a few boys eager to conquer an American on holiday. But, since that fateful moment at the park when she saw Paddy for the first time, she could think of no one and nothing else.

Now, he sat next to her with the stench of beer on his breath and too much cologne. Ingrid felt a dual sense of attraction and repulsion. She wished they could be alone, under better circumstances, to talk and get to know one another. Paddy and Ciaran seemed to be inseparable. Ciaran, to Ingrid, was also insufferable. He had proven in the brief time she had known him to be so different from his other family members. Ciaran was loud, a braggart, and foolhardy one moment then withdrawn and spooky the next. He spoke as if he was the expert on every subject and he seemed to have a temper. While Paddy was quiet and appeared more passive, Ciaran was the Northern Irish equivalent of Becky Harken. He was a bully to his sister and to others. Ingrid hoped he would get a comeuppance. Ciaran reminded her more and more of Clooney.

"Get out of here!" yelled Siobhan. "We want to watch this movie!"

"We're going!" stormed Ciaran.

With that, the boys hurriedly left the room. Paddy had used Ingrid's right leg as support for his left hand as he lifted himself off of the couch. The imprint of his fingers on her flannel pajama bottoms remained and she stared at it. He had looked back at her before departing and, when their eyes met, Ingrid felt at peace again despite the tumult between her cousins. She could not believe that three weeks had passed since they had last seen one another and she resolved not to let that happen again.

It was now Thursday, June 18. There had been so much sad news in Northern Ireland during her visit thus far that, for all of her thoughts of Paddy, she had little chance to mourn his invisibility. Each day someone from the Catholic side or the Protestant side was either shot, maimed, or killed. Ingrid was learning more and more about the Troubles here. Four hunger strikers had died already and she was now more than familiar with the acronyms that Siobhan had listed on the bus ride. She had studied the Civil War at St. Vincent's and now she was living through one. Ingrid wondered if her parents knew in advance of her visit just how dangerous it was in Northern Ireland. They would not have sent her here if they had, that she truly believed, or maybe they did and wanted her to see this for herself. She felt safe with Siobhan at the church, on bike rides, and on runs around the city, but she was gracefully implored by Niall and Mary not to roam very far away from home at night or go out by herself.

One week earlier, eight prisoners had escaped from the Crumlin Road Jail—Gaol in the Irish Gaelic language—in Belfast. They were not a danger to her, Niall assured Ingrid, and she could rest easy knowing that her safety was guaranteed around Lower Falls. She wondered how this could be possible because of the news reports that showed consistent violence in all areas of the city. Each time she saw a British soldier, she thought of Declan. Siobhan had warned her not to speak to any of them and she had followed her cousin's advice. They were everywhere. They had guns. Often, Ingrid thought she was in a war zone. There was such a contrast between her volunteer work at the parish and what she read in the papers and overheard at the pub. Reconciling it was extremely difficult because she had so few facts on which to base her opinion. Like race relations in Louisiana, there were divides in Northern Ireland. Ingrid could simply not understand why faith played a role. Catholic. Protestant. A different skin color. None of it mattered to her.

Two nights later, Paddy appeared at Clancy's with a few of his soccer buddies. Jimmy and Fergal were there, too, but Ciaran was not. Her cousin seemed like a ghost to her at times and it was odd that he would not be with his friends at the pub on a Saturday evening. Ingrid felt like a regular there now and had become friendly with the bartenders. She even helped clear empty glasses on occasion, so the owners would hand her change for the jukebox and she would pick her favorite songs. Paddy sat next to her at the table as his friends got louder and louder. They were arguing about next summer's World Cup in Spain and what squads they should support. Ireland and Northern Ireland were both playing qualifying matches, but the boys showed much more of an allegiance to their southern neighbors than with their home team.

"Twenty-six plus six equals one," Jimmy screamed.

A cheer went up from the pub. Ingrid turned to Paddy to asked him what that meant. He took his right hand and cleared her hair away from her ear, then leaned into her.

"Let's move over there," he said. "I want to be able to hear you."

They stood and walked to a corner table near where the four scary men had sat when she first visited the bar. In the background, Ingrid heard some mildly lewd comments from the other boys but she disregarded them. They were horny teenagers and their friend was leading an American girl to a table to be alone. What else could she expect?

Ingrid thought that this is one of those moments she should always remember and treasure. She surveyed the room, noted that Good Vibrations by The Beach Boys was playing, saw that her pint glass of shandy was half-full, and felt the warmth of Paddy's hand on her lower back. It was like a pleasant dream and so far removed from the crudeness of their interaction on Thursday.

"Why are you here?" he asked.

"Don't you know by now?" Ingrid replied.

The confidence of her own tone startled her.

"I came here to volunteer at the parish and spend time with my family," she added. "But now I find myself spending time with you."

"Good, then," said Paddy. "How long are you going to be in Belfast?"

"About two months or so," said Ingrid. "Just enough time to have my heart broken by an Irish boy."

"I can introduce you to a few of those," laughed Paddy.

"You do that," said Ingrid. "But first tell me what 26 plus six means."

"Oh, you heard Jimmy over there, did ya?" said Paddy. "That's our way of saying there should just be one Ireland. They have 26 counties, we have six. Think that adds up to 32, correct?

"A math wiz," said Ingrid. "My lucky day!"

This flirtation dance was one she had observed in Shreveport before, but had never been involved with one herself. Those were reserved for Team BSD members and a few others. The queens of SVA. She and Laura used to mock these mating rituals. They seemed so desperate. Now, Ingrid was in the fray. She was wholly focused on Paddy and the look in his eyes. There was a childish charm that also had a devilish edge. His were not the black, lonely eyes of Ciaran. They were more welcoming and there was a bit of Cullan's innocence in them. His smile melted her heart. It made her burst. They sat at the table together as two strangers who, oddly, felt familiar with one another. She wanted him to kiss her.

"Well, what's going on over here?"

Siobhan had snuck up behind them and placed her hands on Ingrid's shoulders. It was a loving gesture of checking on her cousin while also finding out the romantic gossip. Paddy retreated. He stood up from the table and leaned into Ingrid again.

"I will see you soon," he promised.

Ingrid turned a shade of red normally reserved for the brightest of roses. Siobhan blurted out a laugh. They were both glowing.

"I think my cousin is in love," said Siobhan. "Isn't that nice? I've been here my entire life and no one has even spoken to me!"

"That's how it is for me in Shreveport," said Ingrid.

"Maybe we should switch places!" Siobhan replied. "I'll find a nice Louisiana boy to marry!"

Ingrid loved the way Siobhan said the name of her state. The cousins were really bonding and had become close friends. She wished Laura were here in Belfast with her. Moira, too. Ingrid imagined the four of them doing girly things together and including Aunt Mary in the mix. Across the bar, she watched Paddy interact with his friends. He was so at ease with them and so at ease with her. He looked back at her and smiled. Then he winked. Siobhan saw the exchange and gave Ingrid a playful punch in the ribs.

There may have been battles going on in Northern Ireland, but Ingrid only felt the beauty of the love planted in her heart that was beginning to blossom.

CHAPTER THIRTEEN

Ingrid had wondered about all of the activity that took place a few buildings to the right of St. Agnes' Parish but, other than the bike tour with Siobhan on her first day in Belfast, she had never ventured west of the church. She had been in Northern Ireland for over six weeks now and was quite comfortable with her adventure. Sunday nights meant phone calls home to chat with Seamus, Kathleen, and Moira. Laura would be there at the appointed time so Ingrid got the chance to speak with her best friend, too. She was writing letters home and receiving at least two a week from Moira. Ingrid missed her sister most of all and looked forward to seeing how much taller she would be in early August.

It was Thursday, July 9. Joe McDonnell, the fifth hunger striker to die, had passed away the day before. So had a teenage boy in the youth section of the IRA. He had been shot by the British Army. There was a tremendous commotion in front of that building at the end of the block, so Ingrid went outside during her lunch break to investigate. The street was filled with people. Many held signs with political slogans. Some were in English, some in Irish, and Ingrid recognized that she was watching a demonstration firsthand. It was just like the ones she had seen on the television news before, but now she was present. She went up to a lady holding a sign in one hand and a baby in the other to ask a question.

"What is that building?" Ingrid asked, pointing it out to the lady.

"The headquarters for Sinn Féin," answered the woman.

Ingrid had heard her father say that term before. She had heard Niall say it. She had heard it on the news. But, now, she was at the political epicenter of the fight for self-determination in Northern Ireland. That's the phrase her father always used. She remembered it now. To think she had been volunteering in the country for a month and a half without knowing that she was so close to the base for a political movement. Ingrid felt a hand on her forearm. It was warm. She turned to find Father McQuarters standing next to her. He smiled.

"Best that you come back into the church now," he said. "A lot going on out here."

"I've never seen anything like it," said Ingrid. "I'd like to watch."

"It's a demonstration now," replied Father McQuarters. "It will be a riot later."

He led Ingrid back up the stairs to the entry of St. Agnes. Some boys were sitting on the steps in awkward stances. It was as though they knew trouble was coming and wanted to be ready to pounce upon it. Father McQuarters gave them a glance or recognition and they dispersed. Better for them to move somewhere else than have him contact their parents over the weekend.

"A lot of people think Sinn Féin is the political wing of the Provisional Irish Republican Army," Father McQuarters told Ingrid. "As a man of the clergy, I refrain from involvement. Many others in my shoes do not."

"It is all so confusing to me," said Ingrid. "The more I learn about the history here, the less I seem to know."

"That goes for us locals, as well," he replied. "I try to teach peace and work for peace, but it is difficult sometimes."

Ingrid appreciated the honesty of Father McQuarters. They had developed a solid friendship since she began volunteering at the parish with Siobhan. He had the persona of a grandfather, or maybe even a loving uncle like Niall, and his insight was matched by his candor and humor. With the political situation the way that it was in Northern Ireland and with the economy forcing many out of work, St. Agnes had become an oasis in the storm of violence and depression. Ingrid was glad that she was able to make a difference, albeit a small one, and felt that working with Siobhan each day was strengthening a bond the cousins would have for life. Even Cullan, her sweet and sensitive younger cousin, had begun helping at St. Agnes.

When she was not focused on her duties, though, Ingrid's mind drifted to Paddy. It seemed that Siobhan could talk and talk to while away their time at the parish, but Ingrid would be lost in her daydreams about him. They had not even shared a first kiss but Ingrid felt that she could give all of herself away to him at a moment's notice. She was excited to meet him again tonight at the pub: Siobhan had already picked out an attractive outfit for her. It was hanging on the door of Ingrid's room and she anticipated the look in his eyes upon seeing it. That was a change for her. Ingrid had begun to recognize the effect her looks had on Paddy, his friends, and men in general. She never got this at home. It felt liberating and empowering. Ingrid was learning that her combination of brains and beauty could serve as an intoxicant for others. She was not a timid, intelligent sophomore existing in the shadows of huge personalities at St. Vincent's Academy now. Ingrid was becoming a savvy young woman in Northern Ireland. And she was in love.

All of the regulars except Ciaran went to Clancy's that night so Ingrid and Paddy were not exactly afforded the opportunity to spend generous portions of time alone. That was fine. It was what they were used to. That was pub life in West Belfast. It was more a gathering of extended family members and neighbors than anything else. Ingrid reveled in it. She loved the singing, the camaraderie, and the craic. That was the term used to describe the exchanges, stories, and gossip among the Irish. Ingrid enjoyed the humor of it all. She loved holding Paddy's hand under the table. She loved listening to Jimmy, Fergal, and Siobhan try to speak over one another. It was a typically festive night and somehow a reprieve from the realities facing Northern Ireland.

The magic would not last.

Mayhem had begun on Falls Road. A peaceful march had degenerated into a riot. Protesters attacked police forces and British troops. Retaliation came in the form of water cannons from personnel carriers and tear gas. Irish republicans threw Molotov cocktails and trash can lids at the authorities. Youths and adults battled one another in the streets. Many of the injured were carried into the pub, which soon became a triage area. Ingrid witnessed bloody faces and broken bones. The anguish and screams were everywhere. Women were beaten, too. Everyone seemed to have a role in the fracas. Paddy grabbed Ingrid's arm.

"I'm getting you out of here," he yelled. "Come with me!"

They ran out the door and turned right onto Falls Road. Siobhan, Fergal, and Jimmy followed closely. The safety of the Fallon's home was just a block away. It would soon be an interminable distance.

British soldiers tackled Paddy and corralled the rest up against a wall just steps from the pub. Their anger and aggression came through in snarling barks of instruction.

"Up against the wall you pigs!" one screamed.

“Shut your fucking dirty mouths!” yelled another.

Paddy, Fergal, and Jimmy were being roughed up. Their heads were pushed into the wall they were facing and their legs were kicked out from under them. Like Declan at the border, they were jabbed and struck with rifle butts. Two soldiers held Ingrid and Siobhan from behind. Their bodies pushed up against the girls in a perverse manner. Ingrid felt that she might faint. Siobhan was combative. She screamed and kicked out at the soldier until he put one hand over her mouth and used the other to punch her in the back of her head. The boys were being severely beaten as the melee raged in the background on the street.

On his feet again, Paddy glanced to his right at Ingrid. Their eyes met. He winked. She was unable to smile but, inside, knew that somehow they would get out of this.

“You don’t look familiar,” said the soldier holding Ingrid. “Where are you from?”

“America. Louisiana,” she gasped.

“Louisiana?” he replied. “Is that in the south?”

“Yes,” Ingrid cried.

“Well, you’re the nigger here,” he snorted.

With that, the soldier began moving his hands all over Ingrid’s body. The young man holding Siobhan did the same. Their grips moved to the chests of the girls, between their legs, under their shirts, and finally on the inside of their pants. Ingrid and Siobhan shrieked with agony. Paddy, Fergal, and Jimmy tried to free themselves to rescue the girls, but they were beaten down once more. The soldiers abusing the girls kissed the back of their necks and pulled their hair. Ingrid was sobbing. Siobhan was no longer defiant. She was numb.

“Why would you be with this scum instead of men like us?” said one of the soldiers.

He kicked Paddy between the legs and then led his troops back into the relative darkness of the street, now illuminated by small rubbish fires and flares. The five of them lay crumpled on the sidewalk, bloodied and molested. Crawling to their feet, they walked the remaining steps to Rockmount Street and got to the Fallon's home. Niall, Mary, and Cullan were waiting for them. They had been watching the news coverage of the rioting throughout Belfast, but they could also hear it and smell the smoke from just half a block in the distance. Mary began to cry. She hugged both of the girls at the same time as Niall and Cullan tended to the boys. Their clothes were torn and bloody. Jimmy had lost two teeth and Fergal's nose was broken. Paddy had taken the worst of the beatings. He was on the floor of the Fallon's living room and was having trouble breathing.

Ingrid knelt down beside him and kissed him on the forehead. This was their first kiss. She felt so dirty and infiltrated. She felt raped. Siobhan's energy had returned and she began plotting her revenge out loud. Ingrid thought about her first image of Paddy playing soccer in the park with his friends. Now, he looked on the verge of death. He motioned for her to come closer to him, so Ingrid put her ear near his mouth.

"I'm going to be fine," he whispered. "If you wait for my lips to heal, I'll kiss you then."

Ingrid started crying. She was so happy to hear this from him, yet she had just survived a nightmare. They all had. The treachery of the soldiers was abominable. Paddy sat up and smiled. His face looked horrible, but to Ingrid he was still the most beautiful boy in the world.

Niall, Mary, and Cullan were continuing to treat everyone when Ciaran came into the house. He looked haggard and tired. His face was red and his clothes were wet with sweat, like he had just run a marathon in jeans and a jacket. Ciaran looked at his friends, Siobhan, and Ingrid then shook his head.

"Why were you all outside?" he asked.

"We were at the pub," yelled Ingrid. "How were we to know?"

"You should have known," said Ciaran. "You should have been smarter."

Siobhan began to lunge at her brother but was restrained by Cullan. Mary stepped between the two.

"We don't need this right now, Ciaran," she said. "I love you both and I'm glad that everyone is safe here now. Enough!"

Ingrid glared at Ciaran. His words had been so unsympathetic considering the conditions of his friends. He seemed to have a bit of an attitude about the situation, as though he knew better. Yet, he had not been home. She made him uneasy. He was too peculiar. Ciaran always wore red socks under his boots and seemed to scratch his legs a lot. This annoyed Ingrid. He would pull up his pants and itch his scabby shins under his socks. She watched him do this and cringed. It was an affront to the manners she had been taught. Paddy forced himself to stand up and faced Ciaran.

"Where were you?" he asked.

"With a new girl," said Ciaran. "I heard all of the noise and came home right away. Well, almost right away."

"We could have used your help, you know!" fired Jimmy.

"Next time, boyos," replied Ciaran. "Next time."

The following day, Belfast would learn that British soldiers shot and killed Daniel Barrett that night while he sat on the garden wall in front of his house. He was 15.

CHAPTER FOURTEEN

Ingrid's phone call to her family and Laura on Sunday of that week was traumatic. Everyone was crying. Everyone was sad. Mary and Siobhan took turns holding Ingrid's hand and playing with her hair as she described to her parents what had happened. Her father sat at the kitchen table in Shreveport hearing his daughters tears, while her mother paced the living room thanks to an extended telephone cord. Ingrid explained that everyone was going to be fine and did not go into detail about the sexual assault. She was too embarrassed and ashamed, especially since it had happened in front of Paddy. Laura and Moira sat on the couch together watching Kathleen's anguished expressions. It was clear to both that something had gone horribly wrong in Belfast for Ingrid, though the degree of severity was not understood by Moira.

When her parents were off the line and Laura was handed the phone, Ingrid burst into tears. She went into detail about all that that happened. Laura began to cry, too, and Kathleen comforted her. Moira sat silently and watched what was happening. She began to whisper a prayer to herself. Seamus was so irate that he walked out to the front yard and just stood there staring at the sky as if a calming answer from above would appear. Kathleen soon joined him and they embraced.

Ingrid asked to speak with Moira. She tried to compose herself before her younger sister got on the line.

"How's it going, Bug?" she asked.

"I'm fine," answered Moira. "Do you like my letters?"

"I love them, sweetie-pie," said Ingrid. "So much. They mean the world to me."

"I'll send more," said Moira. "I miss you."

"Miss you, too, Bug," replied Ingrid. "We'll see each other soon."

Shreveport never felt further away. Ingrid went to her room and got into bed. She did not feel like listening to music, or reading, or doing anything. She simply wanted to heal. The words of the solider rang in her head. You're the nigger here. It reminded her of Becky and Celeste. She felt pity for the solider. Ingrid imagined that in another context she might be flirting with him. What hate had caused his hate? She thought about this vicious cycle. Maybe it was similar to what had always been a part of Louisiana and other southern states.

Ingrid thought that, somehow, her educational preparations would make her immune to the ills of the world. They did not. They only exposed them to a greater degree. She thought of Siobhan's harder edge and of Cullan's sweet, thoughtful nature. She thought of how she distrusted Ciaran. She contemplated the love she felt for Niall and Mary. And, as she was about to fall asleep, Ingrid thought about Paddy. She had not seen him since the attack, though he had left a note for her on the Fallon's doorstep, and she longed for the opportunity to kiss him under improved circumstances.

Ingrid and Siobhan rode the bus to St. Agnes' Parish the next morning. They had missed volunteering on Friday and over the weekend. A call had been placed by Niall to Father McQuarters and he greeted them with hugs and blessings. The anguish on his face was evident and tears formed in his eyes.

"My girls," he said. "My precious girls. I have been praying for you. All of you."

"Thank you, Father," said Siobhan.

"Thank you," Ingrid added.

"You don't have to tell me what happened to you," said Father McQuarters. "But, you can always feel comfortable telling me whatever happens to you in life. Is that a deal?

"Yes, Father," said Ingrid.

He was approachable, accessible, and real to her. The priests and nuns in Shreveport seemed to be on some unattainable plane of devotion. Ingrid liked relating to Father McQuarters. She had told him all about her life at home and he was genuinely interested with the goings-on of her family and friends there. Siobhan loved the man, too, and would often play practical jokes: hiding his gowns and tying knots in his shoelaces were just a few of her tricks.

The girls put on happy faces during that week with the children and the elderly people they were helping. Just working with friendly, smiling folks proved to be therapeutic. It was impossible to mask the bruises, scrapes, and scratches on their faces and necks, but they did their best with makeup and scarves. Cullan had been an amazing asset for the duo. Of all the Fallons, it was Cullan who was most affected by seeing the distress of his sister. He wanted to be a man and protect her, but he was not equipped at that age to do so. Ciaran was not a good influence for him, nor any influence at all with his extensive absences from home. As a result, Cullan would follow Siobhan to the moon and back. He loved his sister and did not want to be far from her side with all of the dangers lurking in Belfast. Having him at the parish as a volunteer made his sister and cousin proud, too.

Ingrid and Siobhan avoided going to the pub that week and the following weekend. They wanted to avoid going stir crazy at home, too, but the political events taking shape were turning Northern Ireland into a powder keg again. They played it safe and stayed inside. Martin

Hurson, the sixth hunger striker to perish, had died on Monday and the International Red Cross had arrived at Maze Prison to investigate prison conditions there. By now, Ingrid had become fully acquainted with the five demands of the hunger strikers. They considered themselves political prisoners and combatants, not criminals. Others did not share their beliefs. She had even heard of something called a dirty protest in which prisoners refused to wash and smeared their cell walls with excrement.

Hunger strikes. Dirty protests. Demands. Ingrid understood why so many people just wanted peace. She had already been ravaged by the war here. Paddy had told her that he was lucky not to be wrapped up in it himself, but she always thought of that first time at Clancy's when he and Ciaran spoke with the four men in the corner. That memory was still fresh in her mind. Who could she really believe and trust when there seemed to be so much secrecy and so much festering beneath the surface? Volunteering at St. Agnes' Parish was her refuge. It was an escape for her, Siobhan, and Cullan. Their work made them feel that they were making a real difference in Belfast.

In the back of Ingrid's mind, though, were two dates that would not go away. The first was her upcoming sixteenth birthday of July 26 and the second was Monday, August 10. The latter was the day she would be returning to the United States. Ingrid was already contemplating how much she was going to miss her relatives in Belfast, Paddy, and the other friends she had met. She loved Father McQuarters and, at the least, knew that she now had another reliable pen pal in Northern Ireland. Ingrid envisioned Shreveport visits by Siobhan and Cullan. The same for Niall and Mary. As for Ciaran, Ingrid did not really have any feelings. He could stay with Clooney and sleep on the house boat.

Ingrid now possessed a collection of cute notes from Paddy to rival those of Moira. She kept them stacked neatly next to one another atop the dresser. It made her feel so warm inside to feel loved by her sister. Similarly, the overtures of Paddy in print were revealing a sensitive boy who had a lot of love to give. He had impressed upon her the fact that this was the first time he had ever felt this way. Fergal and Jimmy had confirmed this, as had Siobhan. Ciaran typically rolled his eyes whenever Ingrid and Paddy were together. She thought him incapable of loving anyone but himself. Often, she found him staring at her and that made her uncomfortable. They were cousins, but perhaps having a new teenage girl in the house—even though Ciaran was rarely there to see her—had some sort of effect on him.

She excitedly reminded her parents during their phone call on July 19 that there was just one more week until her birthday. Ingrid hoped her family had mailed cards and letters in time so that they would arrive before she turned sixteen. After the tumult of the previous week's call, it was wonderful to hear some good news from home. Laura had a date, according to her mother, but she would let her best friend tell her all about it. Moira was painting and memorizing vocabulary words. Seamus won his age group category in a 5K running race. As for Kathleen, she was preparing for a weekday visit to the lake. Ingrid went on and on about her volunteer work and, for the first time—and perhaps inspired by the news about Laura—mentioned Padraig Fitzsimons.

"Our daughter has a boyfriend, Seamus!" exclaimed Kathleen so that the neighborhood could hear.

"Mom!" yelled Ingrid. "Are you crazy?"

Mother and daughter laughed. It was a bonding moment. Seamus rolled his eyes and feigned disinterest. Moira jumped up and down in the background clapping. Kathleen asked to speak to Mary, too, so that she could get some further information.

Later that evening, Paddy arrived at the Fallon's house. He had a single white lily for Ingrid. She had told him that was her favorite flower and about her garden in Shreveport before, so the fact he remembered proved his attentiveness. This impressed Ingrid and, for the first time in a few weeks, she openly blushed. Niall, Mary, and Siobhan gracefully went upstairs to give them space. Cullan was a friend's house and, as usual, Ciaran was gone.

"I want to take you someplace right now," Paddy told Ingrid. "Grab a warm jacket."

With that, she sprinted upstairs to her room. Siobhan heard her footsteps and came to the hallway.

"Well, will you tell me what is going on?" she asked.

"I'm going on a date!" said Ingrid.

"On a Sunday night?" replied Siobhan.

"Any night is good," answered Ingrid.

CHAPTER FIFTEEN

Paddy was waiting outside next to a motorcycle. It had been a gift from his father and had a red gas tank. There was barely room for a passenger on the seat because of a milk crate storage bin at the back end, but Ingrid did not care. She would be closer to him. Paddy directed her to the pegs she should place her feet upon, how she should hold her hands around his waist, and how she should not touch his arms while they were moving. Ingrid had never been on a motorcycle before and had no fear. She trusted Paddy. He had done his best to save her on the night they were attacked. Now, he was taking her on a date. She felt protected and safe and, when the old Honda CB750 blasted out onto Falls Road, exhilarated. Ingrid pulled herself closer to Paddy and held him snuggly. As the sun set behind her, Ingrid looked over his shoulder at the road ahead. There were no protests or riots this night. Instead, open space greeted their approach. For Ingrid, this was peaceful and liberating after being cooped inside the house.

Paddy led her on a circuitous path into the downtown area of Belfast. She noticed a marked contrast from the Irish flags in Lower Falls. Here, the British flag was everywhere. There seemed to be two Belfasts just as there were two Shreveports. At this particular moment, she did not care about politics or anything to do with the Troubles. Her arms were around Paddy and they were whizzing through the streets. Ingrid saw a sign for University Road and soon the pair were by Queen's

University. It was beautiful. She had not seen this side of Belfast at night, only during the day on her jogs, and the lights of the city were inviting to her. Paddy slowed the motorcycle and they rode through the campus until they arrived at the adjoining Belfast Botanical Gardens. The park was closed, but Paddy grabbed a satchel from the storage bin with one hand and Ingrid's with the other. He told her he knew of a special entrance: it was a hole in the fence that they could both fit through.

Once inside, they walked together in the darkness to a clearing by a fountain. The moon was above the Belfast sky now and reflected off the pool of water there. Paddy reached into the bag and pulled out a portable cassette player along with a bottle of champagne. Ingrid was in shock. This was the romantic moment she had been daydreaming about for two or three years. Their faces still showed the effects of the attack by the soldiers, but neither cared. They only saw the beauty in each other at that moment.

"I didn't bring any glasses," Paddy said. "So I hope you don't mind sharing it out of the bottle with me."

"Of course not," said Ingrid. "I'd prefer it."

She caught herself at times to appreciate those moments when she thought she had said something clever. This was one of those times. Her confidence was soaring. Paddy opened the champagne and handed it to Ingrid.

"First sip is yours," he said. "The lady goes first. I know it's not your birthday yet, but I hope you don't mind the surprise."

Ingrid took a drink of the champagne and handed it back to Paddy. It was not exactly chilled and it stung her mouth a little, but she did not mind. The smell of the flowers nearby was wondrous. Loose petals were being cascaded by gusts of wind at their feet. Ingrid gazed at the skyline of Belfast and heard the signal horns of boats on the adjacent River Lagan. It was captivating to her. Paddy turned on the tape player. It was The Beatles. Ingrid had told him how much she liked the band and here she was listening to George Harrison singing *Something* with the boy she adored.

Paddy put the champagne bottle down and took Ingrid's hand to pull her closer. They began to slow dance, under the moon and stars, atop the petals, as the serene sounds of the fountain relaxed their teen nerves. She could feel his breath upon her ears and neck. She felt his hand play with her hair. The world was spinning faster and she hung onto him for dear life. The day when she first saw Paddy playing soccer at the park without his shirt returned to her mind. She wanted to touch him and feel him and love him. Her hand moved to his shoulders, then his chest, as they both pulled their heads back slightly to look into each other's eyes. Ingrid wished the song would never end, but it did.

Into the Mystic by Van Morrison played next. Ingrid's heartbeat increased. She could feel Paddy's warm breath on her face now. Their lips were the width of a hair apart. He kissed her. Their eyes were closed. It was not an aggressive, attacking kiss but a supple, sharing exchange. Ingrid's mind was racing. She was feeling true love for the first time and did not want the moment to end. Paddy pulled her closer. Their bodies were interlocked as they stood next to the fountain. The concepts of time and circumstances disappeared for both of them. It was everything that she had hoped for and she felt like her dreams were coming true for the first time. In a week, she would be sixteen and this was the best birthday present she could have possibly received.

"You're trespassing," came the voice.

The spell was broken. Not by an angry tone, fortunately, but by a security guard who was able to process the scene of the intruders to his garden on a Sunday night with champagne and Van Morrison.

"I'm going to take a ten minute walk that way," said the guard as he pointed in one direction. "Then I'm going to take a leisurely ten minute walk back here to this spot. That's about twenty minutes. Understand?"

"Yes, Sir!" answered Paddy.

The man turned away while Ingrid and Paddy could barely hold in their laughter. It was an interruption to their moment together, not an end. They hurriedly took a few more sips of the champagne and kissed again. There was something about the added danger of having been caught that made it all the more worthwhile, especially since the security guard had turned out to be a hopeless romantic just like them. Their first kiss had been a long time coming. Ingrid did not count the one she had applied to Paddy's forehead when he was on the floor at Siobhan's house. That one was meant to heal, not excite.

Ingrid and Paddy climbed out of the gardens through the same hole in the fence and made their way to the motorcycle. They kissed and held one another before jumping on for the ride back to Lower Falls. The temperature had dropped considerably and there was a thick mist in the air. Ingrid was not concerned. Paddy's familiarity with the route made her feel safe. The roads were slick, too, so Ingrid held on even tighter than before. She felt the heaving of Paddy's chest as he breathed in and out. She wanted to be as close to him as possible. She never wanted to let go. When stopped, he would turn his head to the side to steal a quick kiss. It was Ingrid's first motorcycle ride and her first real kiss and the first time she had been in love. She never wanted this night to end.

There had been serious clashes in Dublin at the British Embassy the day before and over 200 people were injured, but that seemed as far away as Shreveport now. The Troubles were a constant reminder to everyone in Ireland and Northern Ireland of life's brittleness. But here were Ingrid and Paddy, untethered and immune to it all on the Honda as it slithered its way through Belfast's narrow streets. They were able to put the dangers out of their minds. Ingrid felt euphoric. She could not wait to tell Siobhan and Laura.

Paddy pulled the bike onto the sidewalk in front of the house. Mary and Siobhan were peeking out the window and Ingrid caught them. The drapes moved as the two tried to hide behind them, but their shadows were visible. Paddy and Ingrid let out a laugh together that was followed by their grins and concluded with a goodnight kiss. The entire evening had been innocent and perfect.

As the sound of Paddy's motorcycle waned in the distance, Mary and Siobhan pulled Ingrid onto the sofa with them with giddy excitement.

"Details, details, details," beamed Mary. "I can't wait to tell your mother!"

"Neither of you are telling my mother anything," said Ingrid. "I'm really tired and I should go to bed. Big day of volunteering tomorrow."

"I don't think so, cousin," replied Siobhan. "You'll dish the craic now or pay later!"

"He kissed me," said Ingrid.

"Where?" asked Mary.

"On the lips, of course," said Siobhan. "Where else would he kiss her?"

The three erupted into hysterical laughter. Niall had taken Cullan out to get some groceries that Mary had requested for the week, so the women of the house were able to enjoy another moment of uninterrupted hilarity. Ingrid told them about the night with every detail. She was smiling and laughing and felt practically overjoyed. Most of all, Ingrid could not wait another minute to see Paddy again.

She retired to her room and feel onto the bed backwards, but not before grabbing all of the notes from Paddy off of the dresser. Ingrid wanted to read each one of them again. She wanted to replay every second of the night's adventure. Glancing at the nightstand, Ingrid faced a dose of reality: her plane ticket back to the United States. She only had three weeks remaining in Belfast. The treachery of this was painful. Ingrid thought Paddy to be the love of her life, not just a summer fling. She had never experienced feelings like this for anyone before and she did not want them to end. Paddy could not be just a pen pal to her. Ingrid wanted more. She thought she was crazy. Her expectations were out of control.

Ingrid took a deep breath and closed her eyes. She would be back at SVA next month. She would be back walking to and from school with Laura, competing with Celeste, watching the cliques battle one another, playing board games with her sister, and going for runs with her dad. There was no way that anyone in Shreveport, other than Laura, would ever learn about out what happened in Belfast with Paddy. Boys at Jesuit would not understand her newfound confidence or her capacity for love. Her classmates would not realize the depth of her emotions nor the strength of her character. Ingrid was, suddenly, a young woman and not a little girl.

CHAPTER SIXTEEN

The week leading up to Ingrid's sixteenth birthday was very busy at St. Agnes' Parish. Father McQuarters had Siobhan and Ingrid running around like lunatics with the always helpful Cullan in tow. Paddy stopped by twice with lunch and snacks for all of them, which made Ingrid incredibly happy. He worked as an apprentice with a construction company doing odd jobs and, when he had to pick up supplies, was able to find a way to get to Andersonstown. His visits to the church were tempered by the realization that Ingrid would soon be leaving Belfast. Each second together counted. Her departure was not something they discussed. Paddy was quick to let her know that he considered her a lot more than a summer romance. Ingrid felt the same way. He was unforgettable.

Siobhan organized a birthday party on Friday night for Ingrid at Clancy's. A cover band that specialized in Motown hits was going to be there, so the girls were excited about the chance to dance. Mary and Niall were coming, so were Cullan, Fergal, Jimmy, and Paddy plus the rest of the soccer boys and the neighborhood gang. Father McQuarters had promised to stop by for a quick pint, too, so this was really going to be a combination birthday and going-away party for Ingrid. Bittersweet in many ways, but it was the thought that counted and the interest from her new friends was indicative of the positive impression she had made upon people during her short Belfast stay.

The girls did not have to volunteer on Friday, so they spent the day pampering themselves. For lunch, they went to a fish place on Falls Road and gorged on smoked cod, chips, and soda. Ingrid and Siobhan then got manicures and pedicures, ate ice cream, then went home for an afternoon nap. While they were out, Cullan had decorated Ingrid's room with streamers and balloons. Upon discovering the surprise, she grabbed him and planted about a thousand kisses on the boy. Cullan blushed and laughed. He had grown to love Ingrid in the months she had stayed with his family. He may never have said two words to anyone, but he expressed his emotions with his eyes and smile. Ingrid felt that if he could just avoid the negative influence of Ciaran in his life, Cullan would turn out fine. She thought of her own influence on Moira and how healthy that was in comparison. Ingrid felt truly blessed.

They got to the pub before sundown and each ordered a shandy. It had been a beautiful day in Belfast—clear, warm, and peaceful—so the mood in the pub as people arrived was joyous. Niall and Mary came early with Cullan and brought Ingrid a package from her parents along with a letter from Moira.

"Your first birthday gifts," said Niall.

Ingrid knew better. Her first present had been delivered last Sunday night when Paddy had kissed her.

The soccer boys arrived and soon took over the room. They had apparently had a rendezvous at another pub first, so they were well on their way to celebrating Ingrid's birthday. Fergal, Jimmy, and the others took turns giving her kisses on the cheek. She felt overwhelmed and adored. These boys had really become her buddies and, after what she had gone through with the soldiers, her protectors. Fergal, ever the clown, got up on a chair to make a toast.

"Here's to Ingrid, here's to…"

He was interrupted by Jimmy.

"We've heard that one a thousand times," he said. "And I'm supposed to be the horse's ass, remember?"

The boys laughed and slapped hands together. Siobhan had her arms around Ingrid and did not want to let go. She was going to miss her cousin a lot. Cullan gave Ingrid a hug and a rose.

"We have something for you at the house," said Mary. "It's on your bed and we hope you like it."

"If you don't, you're evicted," added Niall.

Ingrid smiled again. Her face hurt from smiling and laughing so much today. She kept wondering when Paddy was going to arrive. He had mentioned having to work on something with Ciaran, but was not sure what that entailed. Ingrid could never understand why the two of them were so close. Fergal and Jimmy seemed like the type of boys that Paddy would have more in common with in life. Both were outgoing and fun and vivacious. Ciaran was a downer. He was always so negative and brooding and, when he was not, he was a bragging chatterbox without anything really to brag about other than bedding local girls that no one else ever saw.

The band was running its sound check and it was a miracle if they could hear a note with all of the noise from Ingrid's party group. Siobhan was holding court, as she often did, and the soccer boys were getting louder and louder in their debates about the best soccer player in the world at the time. That all stopped, however, when the men in the leather jackets and flat caps that Ingrid had seen on her first visit to Clancy's walked into the room. There were only three of them this time and their appearance muted the debate over Maradona and Platini.

"I don't think they're here for your party," whispered Siobhan to Ingrid.

The men took the same corner booth in the back as they had the previous time and the bartender, Eddie, went over to deliver their pints.

"Hope the band is good tonight," said one of the men.

"They're great," replied Eddie.

This particular rough, tough figure had even managed to crack a smile in the exchange, so the soccer boys resumed their debate. It was signal enough to make a little noise and have a little fun without disturbing the three of them. Ingrid was mystified. She had no idea who they were or why people afforded them such distance and respect. After she finished her first shandy, Ingrid decided to find out for herself. She walked over to their table and introduced herself.

"It's my birthday on Sunday and I'm happy you could come to my party," she said.

"Where's your boyfriend and your cousin?" one of the men asked.

Ingrid was stunned. How did they know who she was? How did they know Paddy was her boyfriend? She remembered them talking to Ciaran and Paddy two months ago. Her confidence waned.

"They should be here," Ingrid replied meekly.

"Tell them we need to speak."

Ingrid had turned away quickly without knowing who had said that to her, but she nodded her head to confirm the request as she continued on her path to join Siobhan again. She was too afraid to ask Niall and Mary who they were, but soon saw her uncle raise a glass in toast to one of them from across the room and have it returned in kind by all three.

Ingrid had two weeks left in Belfast and thought she had everything figured out about her surroundings. Now, she felt small again. She felt like an immature little girl. So much was going on that she had no clue about. Who were these men? How did Niall know them? Ingrid was supposed to be enjoying her party yet her mind was racing with questions. Foremost among them was when Paddy would arrive. She really did not care if Ciaran showed up or not.

"Happy Birthday, Ingrid!"

It was Father McQuarters. She was so excited to see him that she nearly tripped over a chair getting to him. Ingrid hugged him and thanked him over and over again for allowing her to volunteer with Siobhan.

"It has been the parish's pleasure," he said. "You are welcome back whenever you wish to return. Frankly, we don't know what we're going to do without you."

"Thank you, Father," replied Ingrid. "You had better be my new pen pal, too."

"Of course," said Father McQuarters. "You'll always be my favorite gal from Louisiana."

An hour went by and the band was in full swing. They played a lot of the Motown hits from the sixties and seventies plus some traditional Irish ballads. The room was buzzing. Ingrid, Siobhan, and the soccer boys were out on the dance floor going crazy. Fergal tried to do the splits and tore his pants! This would never happen in Shreveport. People in Belfast let go. Everyone was dancing and not caring who was watching. Fergal and Jimmy took turns spinning Ingrid and Siobhan around in circles. The group of friends had their sweaty bodies swaying as one to the beat of *Baby Love* by The Supremes, grooving to the music. No one was self-conscious about how they looked because no one was looking at them. Everyone was absorbed with the energy of the moment. Siobhan screamed as her parents started dancing. Even Cullan joined in and he was soon followed by Father McQuarters.

"I didn't know you could dance, Father!" shouted Ingrid.

"This old man still has some moves," replied the priest.

It felt to Ingrid that everything had come together for her on this adventure with the obvious exception of

Paddy's absence. She did not know where he was and she was becoming frightened. It was not so much that he had not appeared at the party yet, it was because she assumed the worst could happen when hanging out with Ciaran.

Ingrid glanced over at the corner of the pub to see Father McQuarters chatting with the three mysterious men. He was smiling, as were they, so it appeared to her that everything between them was fine. Maybe they had attended St. Agnes at some point as kids. But, to her, these were not the type of men who looked like they had ever been children.

The soccer boys were still out on the dance floor hoofing it up. Mary and Niall had returned home, but Cullan was still at Clancy's playing a card game with Jimmy. Siobhan was drunk and looking for a boy to kiss. She kept hugging Ingrid and telling her that she loved her. It was a fun night thus far and still a young one.

Ciaran came into the bar alone. His appearance was disheveled and dirty. He looked like he had been wearing and sleeping in the same clothes for two or three straight days.

"Happy Birthday," he said to Ingrid.

"Where's Paddy? she asked.

"I don't know, little girl," replied Ciaran. "I'm not his babysitter."

She wanted to slap him. Ingrid felt enraged. She turned and ran to the bathroom. She needed to cry, just for a moment, to clear her head. Siobhan followed her and the girls shared a hug together in a stall.

"He is the worst person in my family," said Siobhan. "The worst."

"He's like Uncle Clooney," replied Ingrid. "Just awful."

The cousins hugged again then used to tissue to wipe away each other's tears. They fixed their makeup, then went back to the party in the pub, but Ciaran had already departed. He had taken Cullan with him. Siobhan asked Fergal and Jimmy if they knew where the two were going, but both shook their heads. They had not even noticed Ciaran showing up. Father McQuarters came to the girls and asked what was wrong.

"Ciaran took Cullan away from the party," said Siobhan.

"I'll keep an eye out for them," replied the priest. "Cullan makes good decisions."

"But Ciaran does not," said Ingrid. "Cullan is a sweet boy and we don't want him hanging out with his brother."

"Difficult to stop that in Belfast," answered Father McQuarters. "It seems that brother after brother make the same choices. Sometimes whether they want to or not."

He said his goodbyes then left Clancy's. There was still no sight of Paddy. Ingrid had his family's home phone number, but he was never there so calling would be a waste of time. She did not want to leave her party since everyone else was having such a blast, but that is what she would have to do to make the call from the Niall and Mary's home.

Soon after Father McQuarters had departed, the three toughs in leather jackets got up to leave. The soccer boys cleared out of their way as the men made their way across the floor to the exit. Siobhan winked at one, but her offer of civility went unnoticed. Ingrid just stared at the presence they commanded. It was frightening and impressive at the same time. She wondered what their involvement was with Paddy and Ciaran. And with Niall. And with Father McQuarters. She pulled Jimmy aside.

"Who are those men?" she asked.

"You don't ask those questions," he replied. "If they want you to know, they will let you know."

"Come on, Jimmy," said Ingrid. "You can trust me. I'm leaving in two weeks."

"A lot can happen in two weeks, sweetheart," said Jimmy. "That is what we live with around here. Me? I just like to play football and drink ale and chase birds. Don't catch many, but I try."

Ingrid laughed. For the moment, he had calmed her fears. She could not believe that Paddy would stand her up on her birthday, but she was willing to give him the benefit of the doubt. Maybe he had another surprise in store for her. She hoped that would be the case.

CHAPTER SEVENTEEN

Ingrid was deep into a sound night of sleep in her bed after the party when she felt a hand upon her. It was cold and rough on her right shoulder and moved clumsily under the strap of her tank top. Another hand was soon covering her mouth before she could scream. The legs of the dark figure straddled her hips. At first, she was not sure if this was really happening or if it was just a bad dream. She inhaled through her nose and took in the stench of body odor, whiskey, and clove cigarettes.

It was Ciaran. He grabbed her breasts forcefully then put his hand between her legs. Ingrid jerked her head away and screamed. He slapped her across the face and ripped one of the pockets of her pajama bottoms. Ingrid's lip was cut and a small stream of blood flowed to the pillowcase. Ciaran put his hand over her mouth again, but this time Ingrid was able to bite it with all of her might. Ciaran groaned.

"You bitch," he said. "You fucking bitch."

They could see each other's eyes. Ciaran's seemed recessed and rolled back into his head like a shark during the attack. The momentary pause in the assault was an eternity.

Then they heard the explosion.

It was loud enough to shake the house. Ciaran jumped off of Ingrid, sprinted down the stairs, and ran out the front door. Siobhan leapt into Ingrid's room and turned on the light. Niall yelled for everyone to get downstairs, so the girls moved to the living room and Mary came down from the loft. No one had heard Ingrid scream.

"What happened to your lip?" Niall asked Ingrid.

"You're bleeding," said Siobhan.

"Where's Cullan?" asked Mary.

"He can sleep through anything," replied Siobhan.

Ingrid said nothing. She was in shock. Mary guided her to the kitchen table and cleansed her wound. She rubbed Ingrid's shoulders and hugged her. Everyone was confused.

Residents of Rockmount Street poured out of their homes. So did the residents of Rockdale Street, Rockville Street, and Rockmore Road. They all moved to Falls Road then turned right. One block ahead was the burning carcass of a sedan. Fire and smoke streamed into the sky. A few men were close to the vehicle trying to determine whether there were any possible survivors inside, but the heat keep pushing them back. There were two dead bodies on the ground within about fifteen yards of the car. Ciaran was not among the onlookers.

Niall had gone outside with many of his neighbors to check on the situation with the blast. There had been so many car explosions of late in Northern Ireland and Ireland. None had been so close to his home. As he joined the crowd across the street from the car, the first emergency vehicle sirens could be heard in the distance. One of the men who had been near the dead bodies approached the gathering crowd. It was Eddie, the bartender from Clancy's. He had been cleaning up at the pub and was the first person on the scene.

Eddie was looking for Niall Fallon. Cullan was dead.

There were no immediate explanations as to why Cullan was not home in bed or why he was walking along Falls Road with a friend after midnight when the bomb exploded and killed both of them. Eddie hugged Niall and held him snugly. Friends rushed to Niall's side. He asked Eddie to get Mary, then broke from the grips of his neighbors and rushed across the street to be with Cullan. Niall slid down onto the ground and hugged his lifeless son. He was wailing as the tears streamed down his face. Mary ran to his side. Siobhan stood yards away crying and screaming. Ingrid hugged her from behind. Their son was dead. Their brother was dead. Ingrid's cousin was dead. Cullan Fallon was 13.

There was no additional sleep to be had for anyone in the neighborhood. The light of morning arrived too soon, but not long after the bodies had been removed from the scene and taken to the morgue. Two men were inside the car. They were thought to be members of the Ulster Volunteer Force, though no police authorities would confirm this rumor. Four were dead from a car bomb ignited by a timer. Cullan and his friend, Richard Brennan, were seemingly innocent victims in the wrong place at the wrong time. No one could really be sure of anything at this point in the Troubles.

Mary and Niall sat next to one another on the living room couch. They were gutted. Ingrid, with her swollen lip, ran interference at the front door by greeting well-wishing friends and neighbors. Siobhan sat at the feet of her parents clutching their legs. Father McQuarters arrived. He prayed with the family and wept. Violence had touched Belfast again. The police came to the house and began their inquiry. They asked if Cullan was a member of any political organization. They asked if Niall was. They asked if Mary and Siobhan were. They ignored Ingrid and never mentioned Ciaran.

Father McQuarters took over manning the front door. He stood outside on the porch and blessed visitors. There were hundreds of people stopping by to wish the Fallons well. Niall and Mary remained on the couch speaking with police investigators. Ingrid motioned for

Siobhan to go upstairs with her. They went into Siobhan's room and closed the door.

"Ciaran attacked me," Ingrid said. "He tried to rape me."

"I believe you," replied Siobhan. "He has come after me before, too."

"How can all of this be happening at once?" moaned Ingrid.

The girls started crying again as emotions overcame them. In the course of one night, they had laughed heartily at the party and now Cullan was dead and Ciaran had assaulted Ingrid. Siobhan's blood was boiling. She wanted to kill her older brother. He had left Ingrid's party with Cullan and now her younger brother was dead. Siobhan could not breathe. She was hyperventilating. Ingrid comforted her and held her. She wanted to call her family in Shreveport. She wanted to leave Belfast immediately. And, she still had not heard from Paddy. It was like he had disappeared.

It was Saturday, July 25. Ingrid would turn 16 the following day. She did not want to celebrate her birthday. It was the last thing on her mind. Ingrid became frightened even more than when Ciaran was on top of her. She started to think that everything was connected. Paddy, the tough guys at the bar, Ciaran, the bomb. All of it. Ingrid questioned whether this was just a product of her own paranoia after all that had happened during her time in Belfast or a deadly reality. The fact that there had been no sign of Paddy at her party made her long for definitive answers. Maybe true history was murky and opaque like a dirty window. She thought about the feeling of dancing with Paddy at the garden by the fountain. She thought about the ride on the motorcycle. She thought about the first time she ever saw Paddy at the soccer field. Ingrid's lips were puffy and sore. This was not the first time in her life that she had been attacked by a family member.

Ingrid could not wait any longer. She called her parents. It was 2:00 a.m. in Shreveport and Seamus was groggy when he answered the phone. He knew his daughter would not be calling at this hour were it not an emergency, so he placed his hand gently upon Kathleen to wake her.

"Daddy," said Ingrid. "Cullan is dead."

"What?" answered Seamus.

"Cullan is dead," she replied. "He was killed by a car bomb tonight. He was walking along the side of the road when it went off. It was just a few blocks from the house."

"Are you okay? asked Seamus.

"Yes, I'm fine," said Ingrid. "So much has happened. There is so much to tell you."

"I love you, Ingrid," said Seamus. "Mom wants to talk to you. Hold on."

Mary took the phone and, upon hearing her greeting, Ingrid burst into tears. She could barely speak to respond to her mother's questions. Seamus took the phone from his wife and asked Ingrid if he could speak to Niall.

"Hold on," she said. "I'll get him."

Nothing had changed in the scene downstairs. Niall and Mary were still together on the couch and Siobhan was on the ground with her head resting on their legs. Ingrid told her uncle that Seamus was on the phone and Niall got up to take the call. She ran upstairs to hang up the other line. When she returned downstairs, Paddy was standing in the living room. His face was ashen. She saw fear and trepidation in his eyes. Gone were the loving smile and tenderness of his features; Paddy appeared to have been suffering the same traumatic nightmare as Ingrid and her family. She moved to him and he extended his arms. Ingrid collapsed into his chest, burying her face and tears into his jacket. Paddy held her tightly and squeezed her with all of his might. She did not want him to see her cracked and swollen lips, but he pulled back to look into her eyes and his face immediately reddened.

"What happened? he whispered.

"Ciaran," said Ingrid.

"When?" asked Paddy.

"Right when the bomb exploded."

Paddy went to the couch to hug and kiss Mary. He placed his hand on Siobhan's shoulder and kissed her forehead. Niall was standing in the kitchen speaking in hushed tones to Seamus on the phone, so Paddy went to give him a hug. The two embraced. Ingrid could see her uncle's face over Paddy's shoulder and it looked stained with tears like the tributaries of a river.

Ingrid led Paddy to Siobhan's room. They closed the door and got onto the bed together. She never wanted to touch the bed in the other room where Ciaran had attacked her.

"Why didn't you come to my party?" begged Ingrid. "Why?"

"I have no response to give you," answered Paddy. "You wouldn't understand."

"Yes, I would," said Ingrid. "I would. You have to trust me. You can trust me."

"I can't trust anyone," said Paddy. "You don't understand. Please tell me what happened with Ciaran."

"I woke up and he was on top of me. I tried to fight him off and bit his hand. He slapped me. It hurts so much."

Paddy squeezed her tighter and touched her lips with his thumb. Then he kissed her cheek.

"I can't believe Cullan is dead," he said. "I just can't believe it."

"Why did this happen?" asked Ingrid.

"Why does anything happen?" replied Paddy. "I'm going to try to fix things."

“What are you going to do?” moaned Ingrid. “I can’t lose you, Paddy. I can’t. I’m only here for two more weeks. I can’t lose you.”

“I know,” he said. “ I just have a terrible feeling that I know what is going on and I have to do something about it.

It had been an abysmal night and morning since the party. Ingrid and Paddy fell asleep in one another’s arms. They were locked in a love embrace that only happens when one heart is willing to give everything to another. On Falls Road, crews were cleaning the debris from the explosion. The car and the bodies had been transported away hours ago. Niall, Mary, and Siobhan remained downstairs holding each other and praying with Father McQuarters. Flowers and plates of food were barricading the steps to the front door of the house.

It was the eve of Ingrid’s sixteenth birthday and she was finally in the arms of a boy she loved.

CHAPTER EIGHTEEN

The Irish specialize in wakes and funerals. They specialize in mourning. Relatives, friends, and neighbors have perfected the art of cleaning the family home of the departed and then cleaning it again several times. Everyone has a part to play. Some are too willing. Some become caricatures of themselves: drinking excessively, flirting, and resurrecting past vendettas. In many ways, death brings out the best and the worst in people but reactions seem to get amplified with the Irish. A line tends to get crossed. On one side, there are the true mourners gathering out of respect and remembrance for the dead. On the other, those who use the opportunity to illuminate the rationales and mantras of their own lives.

For several days after Cullan's death, the Fallon's West Belfast neighborhood was numb. No one played soccer in the park, or selected songs at the pub's juke box, or went for evening walks. Mary and Siobhan had not left the house. The only times Niall stepped outside were to claim his son's body at the morgue and make the funeral arrangements with Father McQuarters. He had also visited the family of Richard Brennan to pay his respects.

Ciaran finally returned home on Saturday night. He was greeted with warmth by his parents and snubbed by Siobhan. Ingrid would not look at him or talk to him. Niall asked him if he knew anything about the bombing, but Ciaran said that he did not. He asked where his sons had gone after the party. Ciaran told him that Cullan had followed him to a party in Andersonstown, had seen Richard Brennan there, and that the two left together. This was the last time, Ciaran said, that he had seen his brother.

On Sunday, Ingrid turned sixteen but there was no celebration. Niall, Mary, and Siobhan all wished her well, but they could not be expected to smile. She wore the present they had given her, an Aran cardigan sweater, out of respect for her relatives. Later in the morning, Ingrid went for a run by herself and found a spot in Milltown Cemetery to meditate. She did not really know how to meditate, but she wanted to try to clear her mind and take herself away from the tortures of Belfast. Ingrid watched the passing cars on the M1 motorway in the distance. She touched her face and felt her sliced upper lip. Ingrid's thoughts drifted to home and the lazy summer days she had spent in Shreveport in the past. Maybe there was something to be said for doing nothing if doing the opposite meant calamity, violence, and death. She gritted her teeth. She remembered biting Ciaran's hand and how she could not wait to brush her teeth and shower after his attack. Ingrid had felt her cousin's stares upon her for several weeks, but she never knew that would translate into a drunken attempt at molesting her. Ingrid thought that Ciaran and Clooney were the same. She closed her eyes and felt like she would vomit.

Returning to the Fallon's home, Ingrid was amazed by the amount of food and flowers spread around the living room and kitchen. She thought that most of it would surely go to waste. Father McQuarters had offered to take some of it for his outreach program, so Siobhan had helped him pack up the church van earlier in the day. This made Ingrid smile. Their volunteer work at St. Agnes had been so rewarding and beneficial. It was a stark contrast to all of the misery.

That evening, Ingrid made her weekly call home to Shreveport. Laura was there to chat again and had been briefed about the death of Cullan. So many things had happened since her arrival nine weeks ago on May 25. Ingrid felt like she had lived three lifetimes in two months.

This would be her longest phone call of the summer. She spoke at length with her mother and father about all that had happened at her birthday party, about Cullan, and about Paddy. She told them about Father McQuarters and the love she felt for Siobhan. Ingrid tried to explain the feelings she had about being in the house and experiencing all of this emotion with Niall and Mary. She did not mention Ciaran.

Laura got on the phone and wanted to hear all about Paddy. Her best friend was excellent at finding the silver lining for bad situations, but this time even she could not break through the agony in Ingrid's heart. There was something very different in Ingrid's voice, Laura thought, as if she wanted to express herself but could not find the proper vocabulary. That had never happened before. Laura sensed something was wrong with her in addition to Cullan's death, but she did not want to press Ingrid for more information with Seamus and Kathleen sitting nearby.

Ingrid spoke to her mother again and asked about Moira.

"She's been quiet for the past few days," said Kathleen. "Kind of acting out of character. Maybe it's a phase."

"What's wrong? asked Ingrid.

"You have enough to worry about there, honey," answered Kathleen. "She'll grow out of it. She has been behaving strangely since we got back from the lake."

A chill went down Ingrid's spine. She felt cold. Colder than she had been on the motorcycle ride through Belfast with Paddy. Colder than she had been in a long time. She asked to speak with Moira.

"Still in her room this morning," said Kathleen. "You can talk to her next week."

"I want to talk to her now," barked Ingrid. "Please."

Kathleen yelled for Moira to pick up the phone in the hallway upstairs, but there was no answer, so she sent Laura to check on her. Knocking softly on Moira's bedroom door as she opened it, Laura found the girl on her bed drawing with colored pens.

"Your sister wants to speak with you," said Laura. "She's going to be home in two weeks!"

"I know," said Moira.

The response sounded cold to Laura. Moira was typically the life of the party and full of energy. Maybe she was sick. Moira got off of her bed and walked to the phone in the hallway. She picked up the receiver and Kathleen hung up downstairs.

"Ingrid?" she said.

"Yes, Bug, I'm here," replied Ingrid.

"I want you to come home now," said Moira.

"I know you do. I want to as well. Less than two weeks away."

"Please come home now," implored Moira.

"I'll be home before you know it," said Ingrid.

"I wish it was today," replied Moira.

Ingrid heard the tenseness in her sister's voice. It sounded so familiar.

"Can I ask you something, Bug?" said Ingrid.

"Yes."

"Did something happen at the lake?" asked Ingrid.

"Yes," answered Moira.

"Do you want to talk about it?"

"No," replied Moira, faintly.

"I'll be there to take care of you soon, okay?" said Ingrid.

"Okay."

Ingrid said goodbye, put down the phone, and wept.

She had to get fresh air. It was now Monday, July 27. Ingrid took the bus to St. Agnes and met with Father

McQuarters. Earlier in the summer, she had helped arrange services for two or three elderly people in the parish who had passed. Now, she was assisting with the program for her cousin. Her priorities had shifted so many times in the past three days. Ingrid's entire focus was with Moira. She suspected the worst had happened at the lake house. She wanted to be there for her sister. She wanted to solve all of the problems for the Fallons in Belfast and Shreveport. Ingrid felt powerless.

Paddy came to visit her at the church. He had stopped by the Fallon's home and Siobhan told him to where to find Ingrid. Ciaran was not there.

"I need to speak with your brother immediately," he had told Siobhan.

"We all do," she replied.

Ingrid and Paddy went to the flower garden behind the church. They sat on a bench and held hands. Their worlds had changed so suddenly since the first date and first kiss. Her lips had begun to heal and Paddy leaned over to kiss her. His touch made her heart burst again. Paddy's complexion had returned to normal since Sunday morning. There was color in his cheeks and eyes again. His face was not bloodless or sallow. Paddy kissed Ingrid softly on the lips, on each of her cheeks, on her chin, her forehead, and again on her lips. He held both of her hands. Ingrid's eyes gazed deeply into his.

"I wanted to see you at my party so badly," she said. "I was so hurt. And then to have Ciaran attack me and Cullan die, all at the same time. I don't know what to think."

"I'm going to take care of Ciaran," answered Paddy. "I'm just trying to figure out how to do it."

"There are things I need to take care of at home now, too," said Ingrid. "I'm just trying to figure out how to do that."

"What happened?" asked Paddy.

"Something happened to my sister," replied Ingrid. "Something that I have to fix."

Father McQuarters entered the courtyard.

"Sorry to interrupt you two, but I need some help."

The church van was stocked full with a second load of food and flowers. Ingrid and Paddy unloaded it into the parish kitchen and arranged it into portions for delivery. She knew that the elderly people on her route would enjoy the surprise of a few flowers with their meals and that brought a smile to her face. Working hand-in-hand with Paddy did, too. She wanted to spend every waking moment with him until her plane left the airport.

Her mind raced with thoughts of being alone with him and kissing him again. Ingrid wondered when and where their goodbye kiss would take place. She had so much love in her heart for Paddy. She had so much hate in her heart for Ciaran and Clooney. Ingrid thought of her conversation with Moira. The anguish in her sister's voice reverberated in her ears. She knew this tone. It had been hers just a few years ago.

CHAPTER NINETEEN

Irish wakes are more like rolling wakes: they last several days. That is what was happening at the Fallon's home. Cousins and other distant relatives had arrived from Omagh and Derry in Northern Ireland, and Kilkenny, Galway, and Dublin in Ireland. The postman had to make three trips to drop off all of the condolence cards on this first day of the week. The front porch of the house was piled with another round of food dishes, candy, and flowers. Deliveries from well-wishers never ceased. The funeral was scheduled for Wednesday. Cullan's burial would be at Milltown Cemetery. It was a repository for victims, innocent and otherwise, of the Troubles. Bobby Sands was buried there.

Ingrid tried to spend as much of her time as possible at Siobhan's side over the course of the Monday and Tuesday. Ciaran would make an appearance for ten or fifteen minutes then disappear into the Belfast streets again. Ingrid wished he would disappear for good. She kept imagining what might have happened to Moira at the lake house. There was so much drama in her life. Ingrid had come to Belfast as a virginal girl of fifteen and would be leaving as a ravaged war veteran of sixteen. She thought about the social scene at St. Vincent's Academy. She thought about Mrs. Morton's assignment. Mostly, she thought about the simplicity of her former life and how her outlook in Shreveport would never be the same again. She was weeks behind in her diary entries.

Ingrid had flashbacks to the assaults by the British soldiers and Ciaran. She recalled the showering of kisses she had applied to Cullan and of Becky Harken calling Celeste Wilson a *dumb black bitch.* Ingrid remembered the soldier saying *You're the nigger here* to her.

She wanted to get away, yet felt an overwhelming sense of responsibility to her family in Belfast and to Father McQuarters at the parish. The arrival of other relatives had made her role less prominent but she wanted to be there for Siobhan in any capacity. They shared the horror of an attack by Ciaran. Ingrid imagined that he had gone at his sister more than once. She hoped this was not the case.

Ingrid missed Paddy. It had been two days since he helped her at the parish and promised to see her on Tuesday. Now, she sat on the edge of Siobhan's bed with her cousin's head on her lap. Ingrid ran her fingers through Siobhan's hair and braided it over and over again. The only sounds in the room were their breaths and sobs. Since Saturday morning, Ingrid had slept in the same bed with Siobhan. She could not bring herself to return to the room she had been using other than to retrieve clean clothes.

There were so many people on the first floor of the house. Ingrid had met all of the relatives but could hardly remember any of their names. In fact, she could not remember anyone's name. She did take note of the fact that many looked like Niall and Mary, while a few looked like her own father. Ingrid would be the lone representative of her immediate family at the funeral. It would have been ridiculous for Seamus, Kathleen, and Moira to fly over together—no matter the sentiment involved—and Ingrid did not want them to, either. She wanted Belfast, with all of its imperfect memories, to be her and hers alone. She wanted to mourn Cullan with Siobhan, Niall, and Mary.

There was a knock on Siobhan's bedroom door. It was Paddy. He had come to see Ingrid as promised.

Paddy sat on the bed next to her. He hugged Siobhan and kissed Ingrid on the cheek.

"I'm sorry," he said. "I'm truly sorry."

"Thank you," said Siobhan. "Cullan liked you a lot."

Paddy looked at Ingrid and motioned for her to get up. He wanted to take her someplace.

"I think we're going to go out a bit," Ingrid said to Siobhan. "Can we get you anything?"

"No, I'm fine," said Siobhan. "Just be careful. Please."

Ingrid hugged and kissed her cousin then followed Paddy down the stairs while holding his hand. She felt better already. She got lost in him. It was his smile, his eyes, the grip of his hands, and his embrace. They jumped onto his motorcycle and sped off together.

"I'm taking you to a different pub," screamed Paddy over his shoulder as they turned right onto Whiterock Road off of Falls Road. "We need a change of scenery."

"Thank you!" yelled Ingrid.

They made another right at Springfield Road, a left on Lanark Way, and then a right on Shankill Road. Ingrid had heard of that street before. Shankill Road. She could not piece together where she had heard it—her brain was fried with all that had occurred—but she knew that it was not from a positive story. Paddy guided the Honda quickly down the street, under a motorway, and onto North Road. Ingrid lost track of the street signs after that.

"We're going to the oldest pub in Belfast," said Jack. "McHugh's. You'll love it."

"I hope so," answered Ingrid.

McHugh's was founded in 1711. It had survived German bombing raids and present day civil unrest. Like the botanical gardens, it was very close to the River Lagan.

Paddy and Ingrid entered the bar holding hands. It seemed that they were a world away from the site of the explosion, St. Agnes' Parish, and Clancy's. Tomorrow, they would be attending Cullan's funeral. For Ingrid, entering McHugh's was like walking into the Fallon's home on Rockmount Street for the first time. She had no idea what to expect. Nor did she care. She still felt numb from the soldiers' assault, Ciaran's treachery, Cullan's death, and Moira's apparent incident at the lake house. She needed to feel the warmth of Paddy's body next to hers.

They went to the back of the bar and sat at a booth. Paddy ordered them two pints of ale and, upon arrival, he offered a toast.

"To my girlfriend, Ingrid," he said. "The prettiest girl in Northern Ireland."

Ingrid blushed. She felt special again. It was as if they were in their own world at the moment and all of the pressures outside had been made invisible. She knew, however, that tomorrow would be another dose of reality.

She liked this bar. It had old world charm and was playing great music. Ingrid loved The Pretenders and started to sing out loud.

Oh, but it's hard to live by the rules
I never could and still never do
The rules and such never bothered you
You call the shots and they follow...

She also loved that Paddy was sitting next to her in the booth and not across the table. He had his hand on her thigh and was massaging it. She had never felt such butterflies in her stomach.

"We'll be safe here," he said. "There are some other places around here where we wouldn't be, but McHugh's is fine. Relax."

"I want to feel safe with you," she replied. "I do."

They finished their first round of beers and ordered a second. Ingrid wondered if she would feel comfortable having an occasional pint in front of her parents. The drinking age in Louisiana was eighteen. She felt that she could pass for that now.

Paddy kissed her neck. He kissed her ears. She could feel flushness in her face as though it was being subtly pricked by a million soft needles. Ingrid turned to him and their lips met. Their mouths opened and their tongues teased one another. She thought it was perfect. His hand gripped her leg with more ferocity than earlier. Ingrid wanted to be touched. She wanted more, too. There were plenty of people at McHugh's but no one seemed to notice the young lovers making out in the booth. Ingrid felt like she was flying. Soaring, really, far up above the clouds and far away from the Troubles in Northern Ireland. Theirs was a timeless, limitless connection. She never wanted this moment to end, but it would. In twelve days, she would be on a plane back to the United States.

They left McHugh's and climbed aboard the motorcycle for the ride back to West Belfast. Ingrid could not remember the last words that they had said to each other in the pub. All of their communication had been through touching and feeling. Her body had never reacted that way with anyone before. She felt a bit embarrassed, but that went away once the chill of cold air hitting her face began. Ingrid turned her head to the side and burrowed it into the back of Paddy's leather jacket between his shoulder blades. Her fingers slipped under the jacket and under his shirt. She wanted to feel his skin. Ingrid moved her hands along his sides and to his stomach. She hoped he would be able to concentrate on the road. Paddy felt strong, solid, and warm. Ingrid's heart was beating fast and she determined that this was what true love meant.

Paddy kissed her goodbye at the Fallon's doorstep and went home. It was past eleven and everyone was asleep. Ingrid went up the stairs and climbed into bed with Siobhan. She wanted to tell her everything, but did not want to wake her up. She had. Siobhan rolled over to face her cousin.

"Did you have sex?" asked Siobhan.

"NO!" said Ingrid. "God, Siobhan, we just kissed."

"Where do you think kissing leads?" replied Siobhan.

The girls giggled. They had not done so together since the party at Clancy's on Friday night. It felt refreshing to laugh even though they would be burying Cullan in a few hours. Ingrid had her release at McHugh's with Paddy, but Siobhan had been sequestered in the house playing the role of good daughter and sister for several days. They were not really roles as much as responsibilities and—despite her boisterous nature and zeal with friends—she was still just a teenage girl trying to grow up in a veritable war zone. Ingrid put her arm around Siobhan and the cousins fell asleep spooning together.

CHAPTER TWENTY

The funeral was as miserable as any funeral could possibly be for a boy of 13 with an entire life of promise in his path. Father McQuarters led the mass and service at St. Agnes' Parish, the choir sang, and the procession moved along Andersonstown Road to Milltown Cemetery. Cullan Fallon was buried near other Fallon family members on the southeast field area of the grounds. Lilies and roses were tossed onto his casket as it was lowered. Niall tried to remain strong for his family. Mary sobbed and Siobhan had to be held by two strong Kilkenny cousins to remain standing. Ciaran was, as expected, drunk. He avoided eye contact with Ingrid and Paddy. Fergal and Jimmy cried.

All of West Belfast seemed to be there. Many knew the family, most did not, but the pride of the community and the anger over the senseless loss of two teenage boys was overpowering. It was palpable. Some wanted revenge, but against whom? Two men were also dead and they had families, too. If the bomb had killed two Ulster Volunteer Force members and not two Provisional Irish Republican Army members, then the latter must have set the device that killed Cullan Fallon and Richard Brennan. As often happened after the fact during the Troubles, it was best not to point fingers at anyone.

Ingrid stood amid the members of the Fallon family at the burial. She had gazed across the top of the coffin at Paddy on the other side and tried to smile. He stood stone-faced with a group of boys and men she had never seen before and looked back at her. Ingrid watched as Niall, Mary, and Siobhan walked three abreast, arm-in-arm, out of Milltown Cemetery together. Ciaran walked off in a different direction. Ingrid wondered if he felt any guilt at all about taking his brother away from the party at the pub. The bomb went off five days ago, yet it seemed like years to her. The affection at McHugh's the night before seemed like it happened a lifetime ago, too. So did any memories of Shreveport.

Everyone wound up at Clancy's that afternoon. The soccer boys were there, but no one played any songs on the juke box. Eddie had unplugged it. Niall and Mary sat in a corner booth and accepted salutations. Siobhan roamed the room looking for someone to make her smile. Ciaran came early and left quickly. Ingrid and Paddy stood next to one another and held hands. There was a shrine to Cullan on a table next to the platter of food set out by the pub. Photos of him through the years, a soccer ball, and his favorite Pink Floyd album were spread around a plate of bean dip with potato crisps. This was the quietest Clancy's had ever been. The parents and siblings of Richard Brennan visited and left soon thereafter. They were going to bury their son in Milltown Cemetery the following day.

A reporter and photographer from the *Belfast Telegraph* came to the door of the pub but were turned away by Jimmy and Fergal.

"Not today," said Jimmy. "Not tomorrow, either."

Cullan and Richard were not combatants involved in the struggle. They were innocent kids. The media was not going to exploit their memory; too many martyrs had already been established and demeaned. Their deaths were a terrible tragedy: a classic case of being in the wrong place at the wrong time. It happened a lot on this island. Ingrid and Paddy stepped outside.

"I need to speak with Ciaran," said Paddy. "He's avoiding me."

"What are you going to say?" asked Ingrid.

"I may have to speak with my fists," he answered.

They took a walk up to the park and strolled on the pathway. They passed the field where Ingrid had first seen Paddy playing soccer. So much had transpired since then. Too much. Ingrid felt as if she was having a bad dream. She wanted to wake up. There was so much love and passion for Paddy and, on any other day, holding hands and walking through a park together would have been a magnificent bonding experience. On the heels of a funeral for her murdered cousin was something different. The reality that she would be leaving in less than two weeks was on their minds. Paddy turned to face her.

"We will see each other again," said Paddy. "I promise."

"Oh, you and your promises," answered Ingrid, grinning. "Hope you're a good swimmer. The Atlantic Ocean is pretty wide."

"Someday," he said. "Just don't forget about me."

"I never will," she said.

They held each other and kissed, but it felt different to Ingrid this time. It felt like goodbye.

Back at the pub, the juke box was on again and Fergal was leading the room in local anthems. *The Isle of Inisfree* and *The Wild Colonial Boy* were belted out with power and gusto, though perhaps not with perfect pitch. Niall and Mary had retired to their home, but Siobhan was not leaving. She was drunk and sullen. Several boys tried to turn their hugs of condolence into kisses, but Fergal and Jimmy—as they had with the media hounds—ran interference to defend her honor. Cullan had been like a younger brother to them and Siobhan was, by default, like a sister.

Ingrid and Paddy took seats at a table near the back of the pub. They wanted to be there for Siobhan and also wanted to spend time alone together. It was a delicate balance because Siobhan was stopping by every few minutes and hugging them. Ingrid felt sad. She wanted to stay in Belfast and be supportive of her cousin and be with Paddy, but she also knew that she had to return to Shreveport to support Moira. She had been puzzled for several weeks. Ingrid felt conflicted, but she was also now resolute. Ciaran's attack had changed her. She was not violated like she was by the soldiers during the riot. This was worse. Ciaran was her cousin. His drunk fumbling with her body was uncomfortable and she had tried to defend herself. She got a bite in before being slapped. With the British Army troops, she had no recourses available for protection. Sitting there with Paddy, with all of this fresh in her mind, Ingrid made a personal pledge to herself that she would do her best never to feel helpless in any situation again.

She would be proactive, not reactive. At home with her parents and sister, at school with the cliques, and with her uncle at the lake house, Ingrid would never be silent again. She had taken further steps of empowerment since landing in Dublin. It had nothing to do with turning sixteen. Before, that had been the standard in her mind for the maturity of a young woman. Now, it was not about a particular age.

Ingrid was making a serious life choice. She thought about developing her own motivational quote. It did not matter what streets you were from or walked on in life, she thought, but it mattered what you did on those streets. She liked that. It made sense to her. Ingrid felt the pride of her newfound strength swell in her chest. She leaned over to give Paddy an unexpected, unsolicited kiss. He smiled in appreciation and kissed her back. They were in love and they did not have to say the words to affirm it.

Two officers of the Royal Ulster Constabulary entered Clancy's. Fergal and Jimmy greeted them with hissing sounds. The police were distrusted in most Catholic and republican neighborhoods of Belfast and, for that matter, Northern Ireland. There had been too many cases of collusion between the RUC, loyalist paramilitary organizations, and the British Army. The saying in West Belfast went that for every good RUC officer, there were a hundred bad ones. No one knew into which particular classification these two fell, but an appearance at a pub gathering after a funeral was bad form.

They took a lap around the bar and then did so again. Their uniforms were black from head to toe, as were caps housing an embroidered red crest of a harp topped by a crown. Eddie, who had finished off quite a few pints himself on this day, offered them a round of whiskey shots on the house but received no acknowledgement. The soccer boys sat silently and sipped their drinks. Only Siobhan, in her stupor, maintained an industrious energy level. A song by The Rolling Stones had just ended but she was still singing the chorus.

The officers both took long looks at Paddy. This frightened Ingrid momentarily. She reasoned, however, that nothing could go wrong inside of the pub with so many witnesses. This was the way her brain worked now. She would never have thought that way at home in Louisiana.

Suddenly, Jimmy bolted from his seat and grabbed one of the RUC men's caps. He sprinted out the door of the pub as both officers gave chase. Everyone inside erupted with laughter.

"Well, did you see that?" screamed Siobhan.

Jimmy disappeared quickly around a corner into the neighborhood. He, like all of the other residents, knew the shortcuts and alleyways to get away from trouble. The two officers stood in the middle of Falls Road. One had a cap on his head, the other did not. Another RUC car arrived. Then another. Soon, there were more than ten policemen in front of Clancy's. They were pulling riot gear out of the trunks of their vehicles. Helmets, shields, and batons were now visible to the patrons of the pub and to anyone passing by.

"Not this again," said Paddy.

He still had a smile on his face and looked at Ingrid.

"Stay by my side."

Though they knew Jimmy had left the pub and run off in another direction, the RUC officers entered the room and started knocking over tables. Fergal and his friends jumped back as a baton smashed a pint glass in front of them. Siobhan was pushed to the floor and the photos of Cullan were sent flying. In a matter of seconds, the serenity of a post-funeral gathering had turned into a melee.

Eddie screamed out and appealed for calm, but it only seemed to get worse. Paddy grabbed Ingrid and they ran out the side door onto Rockmore Road. He wanted to get her away from Falls Road and the police presence, so they turned left into the neighborhood and went to the end of the block. Paddy grabbed Ingrid and held her against the furthest brick wall of the last house on the row. He was looked around the corner back towards Falls Road to see if anyone had followed them. Paddy was looking for the police and Ingrid was looking at him.

They heard the shout of a neighbor across the street.

"Get in here," said the woman. "You can get over to Rockmount Street through our back garden."

Paddy led Ingrid into the home and soon they were with Niall and Mary in the living room of the Fallon's house. A short while later, Fergal led Siobhan into the house. She had passed out and he had carried her there. Neither was injured. The RUC had left the pub after doing what they thought was enough damage in exchange for a stolen cap. It was just another example of the way things were in Northern Ireland. A practical joke could quickly turn into national news and provoke condemnations.

Ingrid had not been afraid. In fact, she had been excited. She liked running down the street with Paddy, feeling protected by him behind the brick wall, and sneaking through the home of a stranger to safety. Ingrid felt as though she now possessed some sort of cunning and guile. She had survival skills. Her father had often discussed the *fight or flight* mentality. One had to evaluate the odds of survival in certain situations. Last year, she had not understood what Seamus had meant when he lectured her on the topic at their kitchen table. Now, she did.

Paddy was ready to leave. He did not want to intrude on the Fallons after all that had happened. He helped Niall carry Siobhan to her bed, then gave a hug to Mary and kissed Ingrid goodnight.

Fergal and Paddy walked back to Clancy's to help Eddie clean up. A few others were there, too, sweeping up the glass and wiping down the tables. The damage was not too severe, but Eddie asked Fergal to tell Jimmy to lay low for a few weeks and to get rid of that RUC cap. He actually let out a laugh while saying that, so Fergal let one out as well. Paddy grinned.

It had been a long day. The night would be even longer.

CHAPTER TWENTY-ONE

Paddy needed to find Ciaran. He had so many questions for him. Paddy was confused by the fact that each time there seemed to be an incident, or a riot, or a police action by the RUC, Ciaran was nowhere to be found. He wanted overdue answers.

He had kept many secrets from Ingrid. Paddy was a member of the Provisional Irish Republican Army and so was Ciaran. They were *Provos* and had come up through the youth sections to become full-fledged soldiers. Jimmy and Fergal were not involved. Cullan had not been, either. Niall was the head of an active service unit for the area. Whether Mary or Siobhan knew was unimportant; they would not have said anything if they did.

Everyone was connected in some way or another to the cause. Paddy was worried that Ciaran would get into trouble with the PIRA leaders in West Belfast. It was bad enough that he had assaulted Ingrid. That matter also had to be dealt with, but it was not life and death like one's involvement with the Troubles. Paddy had to answer to the tough men in the caps Ingrid had encountered at the pub. Those were his leaders. Ciaran had to answer to them, too, and Paddy could not continue to vouch for the integrity of someone who was acting so distant.

Paddy knew of several girls that Ciaran was attached to in different Belfast neighborhoods and figured the easiest way to track him down would be to get on his motorcycle and make house calls. His Honda was parked in front of the Fallon's home, so he walked back there again—this time without cutting through a stranger's garden—and immediately discovered a problem.

Ingrid was seated on his motorcycle.

"I'm going with you tonight," she said. "Wherever you are going."

"You can't," answered Paddy. "I have to find Ciaran."

"I will help you," said Ingrid.

Paddy knew better, but perhaps having Ingrid on the back of his motorcycle while he drove around the city late at night was not such a bad idea. She would be a good cover story for him. He could tell any police he encountered that they were on a date returning from a movie and that he was giving her a ride home.

"How long have you been sitting there?" asked Paddy.

"Don't worry about it," replied Ingrid.

She was already bundled up in a warm jacket and gloves. Ingrid loved the smell of his spare helmet when she put it on her head. It smelled like Paddy. Anything to get closer to him, she thought, before she had to leave Belfast.

"You're going to get quite a tour of the city tonight," said Paddy.

"I though you would never ask," Ingrid replied.

"We have a full tank of gas," joked Paddy. "Don't get any funny ideas."

She hugged him tightly as he started the motorcycle. They sped onto Falls Road, past the shops and restaurants that had all closed hours before, and into Andersonstown. Paddy backtracked to Lower Falls, then drove downtown to Sandy Row. That was a heavily loyalist area just like Shankill Road. They headed to North Belfast to look for Ciaran in New Lodge and Tiger's Bay. Siobhan's brother had a flock of birds spread all over the city that was not limited to any particular sectarian zone or interface area. Paddy was determined to find the right cage that night. He wondered why Ciaran had ever felt the need to try to get with Ingrid, his own cousin, when he knew she was also the girlfriend of a fellow Provo and friend.

Paddy remembered one girl that Ciaran had mentioned several times. Her name was Orla and she lived north of the city in the Glenbryn estate area. That was a dangerous place for a young man from West Belfast to be during the day, let alone at 9:30 p.m., but having Ingrid along for the ride would be less conspicuous. Even on a Wednesday night in late July. He looked at her in the rear view mirrors of his motorcycle. Ingrid was smiling. Her skin seemed to glow in the reflection of the mirrors under the streetlights they passed. She was beautiful to him.

Paddy just wanted to locate Ciaran, say a few words to him, then get Ingrid back to Siobhan's house. He did not want to put her into harm's way again.

Glenbryn was adjacent to Ardoyne, a republican area, so at least Paddy knew that he could go a couple of streets over and be safe if problems arose. He was not sure of the exact address for Orla's house, but he had been there once before and remembered that the home was painted yellow. Paddy hoped they had not repainted it. He thought it was either on Glenbryn Parade or Glenbryn Park, so he circled both blocks a few times. Ingrid was not impatient. She reveled in the adventure and just wanted to spend more time with Paddy. Seeing Ciaran in this context would be good for her; she trusted Paddy and knew he would be protective.

Paddy saw the house. It was on Glenbryn Parade: a yellow, two-story home with a dainty garden in front. It was one of the only brick homes on the block that was not red in color. The curtains in the front window were partially closed, but Paddy thought if he got close enough he could take a peek inside. He parked the motorcycle a few houses down form Orla's and asked Ingrid to wait for him.

"I'm going with you," she exclaimed.

"No," Paddy answered. "You're staying here."

"No," said Ingrid. "I am not. If you are going to confront Ciaran, I want to be there."

She did not know about the many other questions Paddy had for her cousin. Ingrid assumed her boyfriend was only seeking out Ciaran to defend her honor.

"Fine," he said. "But you have to be quiet. I just want to look in the window to see if he is there with Orla. Ten seconds max."

She followed him to the yellow house and watched as he climbed a small fence into the front garden. Ingrid could tell there were people in the front room of the home because of the shadows cast upon the drapes. It reminded her of when Mary and Siobhan had tried to spy on her with Paddy. Ingrid waited on the sidewalk. She felt another rush of excitement. She always did with her boyfriend. It was exhilarating.

Paddy stood crouched in front of the window for only a few seconds, but in that brief span of time he witnessed enough to nearly make himself ill. It was not from any sexual liaison between Ciaran and Orla. He wished it had been that. His whole world would not have been turned upside down by watching them fool around on a couch. Paddy could not tell Ingrid what he had seen. He had to lie to her again. As he scaled the fence and met her on the pavement, Paddy took Ingrid's hand and rushed her to the motorcycle.

"Well," she asked. "Was he there?"

"No," answered Paddy. "Just the parents."

By the way he started the motorcycle and sped away so quickly without further explanation, Ingrid doubted that his explanation was accurate. She was correct. It was not even close.

Ciaran was, indeed, at the house. Orla was nowhere to be seen. Paddy saw him sitting on the couch, drinking tea, speaking with three RUC officers. They looked like the ones who had torn up the pub earlier. They all looked the same to Paddy. Ciaran appeared calm and confident with his handlers. He was smiling and laughing. It was as if he was an entirely different person from the one Paddy had come to know playing soccer, hanging out at pubs, and in field training sessions with other young Provos. It all made sense to him now.

Ciaran was a *supergrass*, the term for a traitor in Northern Ireland. He was a spy and an informer. Niall, his own father, ran an active service unit in West Belfast and Ciaran was betraying his blood. He was betraying everyone he knew. Most of his friends were involved with republican activities. Ciaran reported to the same leadership in the PIRA hierarchy. Paddy was disgusted. They were all in jeopardy now. The RUC had to know who they were.

The juxtaposition between his feelings was overwhelming: he felt such love for Ingrid as they rode on his motorcycle back to Lower Falls and so much scorn for Ciaran, his lifelong friend. Paddy was sure that Ingrid sensed something was not quite right. She had. He decided to play it cool and just be himself. It was acting and he felt terrible about it, but it was necessary. Before they made the final turn onto Rockmount Street, Paddy stopped on Falls Road and turned around to give Ingrid a kiss. She smiled and shivered at the same time.

"Are you in love with me, Padraig Fitzsimons?" she asked.

"What if I am?" he replied.

"I hope you are, Padraig Fitzsimons," said Ingrid.

"I hope you feel the same way about me, Ingrid Fallon."

They were in love and they had 11 days left to be in each other's arms. Ingrid kissed Paddy once more then bounded into the house and up the stairs. Her cousin's room smelled about how one would expect it to after the night Siobhan had at the pub. Ingrid grabbed a pillow and blanket to sleep on the floor. She would dream of her boyfriend.

Paddy had other pressing matters. He had gone to confront Ciaran about his whereabouts in the past—and the attack on Ingrid—and received more information than he had anticipated or wanted. Provos had gone missing and never been found again. There were rumors of unit infiltrations by supergrasses all across Northern Ireland and the Republic of Ireland. The RUC had offered substantial payments and immunity from prosecution to paramilitary members in exchange for divulging the identities of their comrades. These, at least, were still just rumors. Even at 17, though, Paddy was experienced and mature enough to know that rumors typically got started because of substantive reasons.

If Paddy approached his leadership with word of the betrayal, Ciaran would be executed. If he told Niall, Ciaran would be banished from his family forever and still possibly assassinated. If his leadership and Niall found out that Paddy knew about Ciaran's dealings with the RUC and did not report it, he himself would suffer stern consequences.

Paddy had to get to Ciaran as soon as possible. He just did not know how.

CHAPTER TWENTY-TWO

Ingrid helped Father McQuarters with the services for Richard Brennan at the church, but she did not attend the burial. She felt it would be inappropriate and, after Cullan's funeral the previous day, she had seen enough. Before she left for St. Agnes in the morning, Ingrid asked Siobhan to join her. She thought it would be a good idea for her cousin to be in the presence of Father McQuarters again, but then felt stupid. The entire day would just be another reminder of Cullan's death. Ingrid reminded herself to think before speaking. Her mother called it the *one-second rule*: take a breath and wait a second before blurting out that brilliant idea in your head to save yourself and others from discovering it not so brilliant.

She decided to walk back to Siobhan's house from the parish after the funeral. All of the homes and businesses she passed on a bike during her first day in Belfast looked so different to her now. Ingrid thought about how Louisiana would look to her when she returned. Years later, in reflecting about this time of her life, she would refer to lyrics in the U2 song *Rejoice* as a guide:

I can't change the world,
But I can change the world in me…

Certainly, her perception of the people, places, and things in Shreveport would be different now because of her experiences in Belfast. Ingrid would not see anything at face value in the future. She would look for deeper meanings in everyday life just as she did in algebra and chemistry classes. As she walked toward Lower Falls on Andersonstown Road and looked at the faces she encountered along the way, Ingrid imagined what it would be like to be in their shoes. Maybe some were Protestant, maybe most were Catholic. To her, the distinction was as unimportant as the difference in skin colors between white and black. Like so many times throughout the summer, she thought of Celeste Wilson and what it must have felt like to have been called a *dumb black bitch.* She remembered the shock of the soldier saying *You're the nigger here* to her. She could not get the two events out of her head. Maybe we were all *niggers* in a way, thought Ingrid, and we should pity and pray for the people doing the name calling.

Ingrid felt the world within her changing. To what degree, however, was to be determined. She could not figure out what to do about any of these situations.

Ciaran was alone in the living room watching television when she entered the house.

"No one else is home," he said. "Just us."

It was the creepiest thing Ingrid could have imagined him uttering.

"Where are they?" she asked.

"They all went out to eat," replied Ciaran. "Had to finally get out of the house or something."

His lack of compassion and understanding of human suffering astounded Ingrid. Ciaran had to be a sociopath, at the very least a narcissist, and he made the hair on the back of her neck stand up in the same way that being around Clooney did.

"Paddy needs to see you as soon as possible," she said. "It's important."

"Ah, yes, your boyfriend," snorted her cousin. "I need to speak with him, too."

Ciaran reached out to a piece of paper and pen on the table near the couch and began scribbling something. Sympathy cards cascaded over the table's edges. There were six or seven empty beer bottles on the ground. He handed the note to Ingrid while looking her dead in the eyes.

"That's where your boyfriend can find me tonight," he said. "Tell him not to be late."

Without reading it, Ingrid folded the paper and placed it into her purse. She did not want to be alone with Ciaran in the house. This was the first time he had said a word to her since calling her a *fucking bitch* during his attack.

Ingrid turned and walked toward the front door. As she opened it, she looked back to see Ciaran staring at her with a blank expression on his face. She found him to be an emotionless pig. Ingrid wondered if he even remembered assaulting her. Was he too drunk? Did he think it was Siobhan in his bed that night and not her? Lingering on these questions would drive her insane. Ingrid wanted to free herself of the memory. But how? Ciaran was another Clooney.

She thought of Moira. Since speaking with her sister on Sunday, Ingrid had been seething with anger boiling beneath the surface of her skin as she mourned alongside the Fallons and fell deeper in love with Paddy. She felt like a one-armed circus juggler with a thousand balls in the air.

Ingrid walked along Falls Road to the park. She hoped the soccer boys would be playing there and when she found them they were a welcome sight. Fergal, Jimmy, and the rest waved to her and she waved back. Ingrid took off her shoes and socks. She rubbed her feet over the smooth blades of grass and dug her toes into the damp turf below. This earthly connection gave her a sensation of wholeness. There was purity in the lawn and its upkeep. There was joy in the athleticism and friendship of the boys playing footie. A few were trying to show off for her with parlor tricks. That was obvious to Ingrid. It was something that she would not have recognized months earlier in Shreveport at a Jesuit sporting event or passing by a group of boys playing basketball in a driveway. She recognized it now. This was the natural order of life.

During a break in the action, Fergal came over to her.

"Seen Paddy?" he asked.

"I'm actually looking for him now," said Ingrid.

"He was supposed to meet us for this kick-around," answered Fergal. "I guess we'll see him at the pub later."

Ingrid pulled Ciaran's note out of her purse and read it. His penmanship was atrocious.

Linfield FC. 9:00 tonight.

She knew that FC meant football club, but did not know anything about Linfield. Ingrid would later learn that the grounds for the club hosted an infamous incident in 1948 when Belfast Celtic FC had its players attacked by Linfield's supporters near the end of a contentious match.

The soccer boys resumed their play and, minutes later, Paddy appeared. Ingrid had somehow sensed his presence behind her. She rose from her seat on the lawn and ran to him, barefoot. He ran to her, as well, and they hugged each other with a ferocious passion. Paddy kissed her aggressively and Ingrid returned his energy in kind. Their hands gripped each other's backs. Their fingers caressed each other's faces and ran through their hair. At that moment, they were the only two people in the park and the only two lovers in the world. Ingrid felt lightheaded and, instead of composing herself, let the intensity of the moment take hold of her. She bit Paddy's neck and ear lobe. He grabbed the back of her neck to pull her closer.

"I love you," he whispered.

"I love you," she replied.

Ingrid felt a soccer ball hit the back of her legs. She jerked her body and Paddy opened his eyes to see Jimmy standing a few yards away from them. The rest of the boys started clapping.

"Hey," said Jimmy. "Do the two of you mind thank you very much!"

Ingrid and Paddy laughed. Jimmy, too. It was 6:00 p.m. on July 30, 1981.

They all headed to Clancy's and, once inside, pushed two tables together so they could sit as one large group. Eddie was behind the bar and everyone seemed to be smiling. *The Cowboy Song* by Thin Lizzy was blasting from the juke box. Ingrid secreted Ciaran's note to Paddy under the table. He read it in his lap then gave it back to her. She returned it to her purse.

"I guess that's that then," Paddy said to Ingrid.

She clutched his hand and smiled. Ingrid was still under the impression that their meeting was to be about the incident she had with her cousin.

"I want to go with you," she said.

"No, not this time," answered Paddy. "This is something I need to do alone."

Ingrid felt sad. She wanted to spend as much time as she could with Paddy before she went back to Louisiana. They had told each other that they loved one another for the first time just steps away from where she had first seen him. Still, she understood that he wanted to protect her and she respected Paddy for that.

The pub broke out into song again. It was barely 24 hours since the RUC men had invaded the bar. This was the resiliency of the neighborhood and its residents. Jimmy had the nerve to reappear the very next day after snagging the cap off of the policeman's head. What did he have to lose? They were working class boys from working class families. They felt persecuted and shunned by the power elite in Belfast. So had their parents and grandparents and generations before. The pub was theirs and they would defend it.

A few people who had attended Richard Brennan's funeral came into the bar. They were greeted with hugs. There had to be some joy found in the week and this was the place to find it. Except, for Ingrid, when slow songs were played on the juke box. They made her melancholy. She wanted to take Paddy with her to Shreveport, but she could not stay here and he could not leave. He took her hand in his again and squeezed firmly. Their eyes met. Each time that happened she felt rapturous.

Paddy's meeting with Ciaran was just a few hours away. Ingrid was already devising methods to be there, too. She asked Eddie how to get to Linfield FC's stadium. It was just over a mile from the pub. She could walk there or ride a bike there. Perfect, she thought. Paddy would be on his motorcycle so she would get a head start. Ingrid wanted to see her honor being defended, by words or fists, even if that meant her cousin was the rebuke's recipient.

Ciaran had assaulted her and she would never be able to forget about it or forgive him.

CHAPTER TWENTY-THREE

A light rain began to fall upon Belfast. It sprinkled down from the heavens and cleansed the dirt and grime off of the streets. Flower petals absorbed its delicate kisses. As Ingrid rode along Donegall Road into Belfast, she felt a blend of anticipation and trepidation. It was the same feeling as approaching the front of a classroom to read an original composition to her peers. Drops of water danced off of her windbreaker as she pedaled faster; she wanted to find a hiding place to watch Paddy's meeting with Ciaran.

She went under the M1 motorway, made a sharp right, then a quick left, and then a right onto Donegall Avenue. Linfield Football & Athletic Club was at the end of the street. It was a dead end. Ingrid found a hiding place behind some trash dumpsters. She figured that they would meet on the stadium side. There were a few streetlights nearby, but from her position she would be undetectable in the darkness of shadows. Ingrid had an excellent vantage point and was proud of herself for stalking the best available position. She felt like a detective.

The meeting was five minutes away from taking place when Paddy arrived. He parked his motorcycle on the other side of the street from Ingrid then stood under a solitary streetlight. Ingrid thought the grandstand behind him looked, in many ways, like a castle. She imagined him to be her knight. Ingrid liked watching Paddy when he did not know she was looking. His striking features grew even more welcoming as he paced around waiting. Her body fit together so well with Paddy's, she thought, like two pieces in a jigsaw puzzle that snap into place after several attempts at making them fit.

A figure appeared in the distance. The man walked from the shadows of Olympia Drive and turned right onto Donegall Avenue. His pace looked faster to Ingrid. She thought it was nervous energy. Or, maybe he was on something. It was not the way an obnoxious and usually drunk person like Ciaran walked.

Ingrid watched as the two friends came together. They did not shake hands. Paddy had his hands on his hips and he was shaking his head. She could not hear what they were saying to one another. The person across from Paddy seemed to be making odd gestures. It was as though Paddy was speaking a different language to him. He kept raising his arms up and down. Ingrid sensed antagonism between the two. Paddy reached out to put his hand on the man's shoulder, but the stranger pushed it away. Ingrid saw her boyfriend shake his head. She saw the man drop his in apologetic fashion. It was not Ciaran.

Ingrid did not notice that the skies had opened or that the intensity of the rain had progressed from a drizzle to a downpour. She did not feel her clothes getting saturated with moisture, nor her sopping wet feet within canvas sneakers. Her complete focus was on the interaction between Paddy and the stranger. She did not anticipate the bike ride back to the Fallon's house on Rockmount Street in the rain, either, and she did not see or hear the dark van approaching.

It coasted toward Paddy and the man, engine and lights off, until it stopped a few feet short of their positions on the sidewalk. The stranger lunged at Paddy. He grabbed his legs and tackled him to the ground. Four men wearing hoods got out of the van and moved cautiously to join in the attack. Ingrid started running to Paddy. Her screams drew the attention of one of the hooded men and he went to intercept her, but slipped off of the curb and fell. Paddy was being struck with fists and boots. Ingrid reached the fight and pushed one of the men. He turned and punched her in the face. She was knocked to the ground.

Paddy was struggling for his life. He fought his way to his feet and warded off the initial onslaught, but five-on-one was never going to be a fair fight. Ingrid raised herself up to her knees and screamed out for the men to stop, but her protest only seemed to worsen the beating.

"Keep your mouth shut, bitch!" said the man without the hood.

Ingrid crawled on top of Paddy, now close to being unconscious from the pummeling, but was pulled off by a few of the men and kicked in the stomach. She felt every bit of air in her lungs explode out of her mouth. The next breath in was excruciating and she fell into a prone position on the cement again. Her head was turned to Paddy as the men started dragging him to the van. She was struggling for air, but had enough energy left to crawl once more toward her boyfriend. She grabbed the leg of one of the hooded attackers just below his knee. He was wearing dark camouflage pants, the type that commandos wear in movies, and black combat-style boots.

The man seemed to kick at her as if he was trying to free himself from a snare trap. Ingrid's hand slipped down his leg and, as it did, the man's jerking motion caused his pant leg to raise. She heard Paddy yell out her name as he was shoved into the vehicle. Ingrid did not want to let go of the stranger's leg, but she could no longer maintain her grip. He pulled himself a foot or so away then kicked out again to strike her in the shoulder. His boot was next to her face and Ingrid's eyes were open.

He was wearing red socks.

Ingrid collapsed to the ground, unable to continue, and watched as the van drove away into the wet Belfast night. She began to sob uncontrollably and scream. Her fists pounded the cement. She cried out for Paddy, but all she could hear in return was the waning sound of a van's engine and raindrops splashing into puddles alongside her body. Ingrid was in shock. Her body had been brutalized again.

And Paddy was gone.

CHAPTER TWENTY-FOUR

She did not remember the nice couple walking its Airedale Terrier named Jack that found her and called for an ambulance. She did not remember the nurses and doctors at Belfast City Hospital that administered care to her wounds. She did not remember Niall and Mary coming to her bedside or being told by Eddie that he had closed the bar early to visit her. And, Ingrid did not remember Father McQuarters saying prayers with Siobhan, Fergal, and Jimmy in her recovery room.

What she did remember was that one of Paddy's attackers wore red socks.

Ingrid was in no condition to give the RUC detectives any credible information other than a bizarre tale of Paddy being beaten and abducted by five men, four of whom wore hoods, then thrown into a dark van. She wanted to sleep forever. She wanted to die. She wanted to go home.

It was late Friday evening on the last day of July, 1981. A man named Peter Doherty would be shot by a British solider on that date while at home in the Divis Flats area of Belfast, not too far from the Fallon's residence. Ingrid had been in and out of consciousness since being rescued. Niall and Mary had called her parents and arrangements were being made to fly her home to Shreveport sooner than August 9. She burst into tears when her aunt gave her that news. Ingrid had wept so much during her time in Belfast—more than in her entire life combined—and could think of nothing but getting home to her family.

Her feelings vacillated with anxiety from fear and numbness to anger. She was furious that Moira had been put in harm's way at the lake house with Clooney. She was saddened by the inexcusable loss of Cullan. She was numb from the witnessing the beating and abduction of her first love. It felt like she was having a nervous breakdown. Ingrid cried out so loudly that three nurses rushed to her side. It was a wounded animal's death wail. A doctor came into the room and administered a sedative. She would sleep well into the following day.

At the Fallon's house, Father McQuarters provided solace for Niall, Mary, and Siobhan. They felt guilty and ashamed for placing Ingrid into their world within the Troubles. She had traveled to Belfast to bond with family and volunteer at a church. The scorecard from her stay was two beatings, the death of her cousin, and the probable loss of her Paddy. Only Siobhan knew of Ciaran's attempts to rape Ingrid. She had not told anyone. Ingrid had sworn her to secrecy.

Ingrid was awakened by a new visitor on Saturday afternoon, August 1. The sleep in her eyes had to be cleared before she could recognize his face. It was one of the men from the pub who always wore a leather jacket and a herringbone flat cap. He was one of the scary men who Ingrid now thought not so scary at all.

"I'm not going to tell you my name," he said. "Everyone around here already knows it, but they don't say it, either."

"You're not going to hurt me, are you?" asked Ingrid. "You couldn't if you tried. I feel like I already died last night."

"Do you remember what happened?" asked the man. "I'm not going to hurt you. I'm going to protect you."

He had piercing blue eyes that looked like a kaleidoscope to the medicated Ingrid.

"They took Paddy," she replied. "Five of them. They took him away in a black van after they beat us up."

"No one is going to hurt you again here," said the man. "I promise."

"I'm going home in a few days," answered Ingrid. "I'm never coming back here."

"Is there anything you remember that might be helpful to us?" he asked.

"I told the police all that I remembered," said Ingrid. "Which wasn't much."

She was keeping one important detail from him, the RUC, and her family. Ingrid did not feel the need to be forthcoming with anyone about seeing Ciaran's red socks.

"Get your rest," said the man. "Paddy was a good boy with a good heart. We know that he loved you."

Ingrid began to cry again. The man patted her forehead and left the room. She remembered when Paddy and Ciaran spoke to him and the others in the flat caps at the pub. It was too much to put together. The possibilities overwhelmed her. She could not change 800 years of history on this island in a matter of months. Ingrid could not resurrect her cousin or reclaim Paddy. She wanted to be at peace. She longed for the moment when her father, mother, and sister would hug her at the airport. Most of all, Ingrid longed for Paddy.

She was in a Belfast hospital and would remain there for two more nights. Over the course of her concussed weekend, Kevin Lynch and Kieran Doherty would be the seventh and eighth hunger strikers to die.

CHAPTER TWENTY-FIVE

Niall, Mary, and Siobhan picked up Ingrid from the hospital on the morning of Monday, August 3. They took the same route back to their home as on the day she had arrived at the bus station in May. Ingrid did not want to go there. She would have preferred to stay in the hospital until her flight. She did not want to see Ciaran ever again. Ingrid had not told anyone about seeing his red socks. She knew he was one of Paddy's assailants. He had set the time and the place for the meeting. It had been a setup—an assassination that involved planning by her cousin—but she had no idea how to react to its aftermath. She understood now that Paddy's desire to speak with Ciaran had more to do with something else than with her.

Ingrid's parents were able to change her flight due to the medical emergency of the attack. She was now going to fly back to America on August 5. Classes started at SVA in a few weeks. She wanted to be a normal teenage girl in Shreveport again: walking home from school with Laura, going to Jesuit's football games, and helping Moira memorize every word in the dictionary. Ingrid wanted to tend the lilies in her yard. She wanted to plant more in honor of Cullan and Paddy.

She knew her boyfriend was already dead.

Ingrid arrived at the house and went directly to Siobhan's room. Mary brought her some tea and Ingrid buried herself under the covers. Siobhan came into the room, closed the door behind her, and sat on the floor. She reached out to rub Ingrid's feet and legs. Her touch was tender and loving.

"We haven't seen Ciaran since Thursday," said Siobhan.

"I hate him," answered Ingrid.

"I hate him, too," replied Siobhan. "But what can I do about it? He's my brother. The only one I have left now. It's sad and pathetic. I miss Cullan so much."

The fact that Ciaran had not been seen since the same day as Paddy's abduction was not lost on either cousin, but neither dared to mention the coincidence.

"Me, too," moaned Ingrid, her eyes welling up with tears again. "I miss Paddy."

The girls had spent so much of the summer laughing and telling jokes together. Now, all they could remember was the time spent holding one another and sobbing.

"I have your purse," said Siobhan. "The people who found you got it and brought the bike back to us, too. That's one piece of good luck, right?"

Ingrid's head still hurt and her body was sore. The most pain, though, was reserved for her heart. It was broken. She wanted closure with Paddy. Her final image of him was when he was being dragged into the van. She thought of that last afternoon at the park and the pub when they kissed, held hands, and gazed into one another's eyes. She remembered the motorcycle rides. She remembered it all.

Ingrid smiled and drifted off to sleep again. She would spend most of the day in bed other than when she showered and grabbed a snack in the kitchen. Siobhan did not leave her side. Volunteering together at St. Agnes' Parish was just a memory for the cousins now. All of Belfast's beauty had disappeared for Ingrid. The colorful murals, the lush hillside scenery, and the smell of the sea at the docks only provided backdrops for her heartaches.

As Siobhan napped on the floor, Ingrid played back the summer like a movie in her head. She felt that she had grown up too fast in Northern Ireland. Her life had been touched by violence, death, and betrayal. Ingrid recalled the lessons of Shakespeare in Mrs. Morton's literature class. This was real life. She had lived it. And, like much of The Bard's works, there was a lot of tragedy.

Ingrid thought of her work at the parish with Father McQuarters. She wanted to spend time with him before she left Belfast. It was peaceful at the church. Ingrid hoped to thank him for everything he had done for her and for the Fallon family. She remembered him dancing at her party and that recollection made her smile. It hurt to smile. She had taken that punch to her face and had the black and blue bruise marks to prove it. There was also an impressive shiner under her left eye, too, that made her look like Rocky Balboa.

At dinner on Monday night, Ingrid asked not to be fed but Niall and Mary forced her to eat. She needed something inside of her stomach to offset the effects of the painkillers, so they fixed her a proper Irish full breakfast for supper: fried eggs, black pudding, fried tomatoes, baked beans, and soda bread. Ingrid cleaned her plate and also asked for second helpings of eggs and bread. She was regaining a bit of her strength and, despite her outward appearance from the beating, would be healthy enough to fly home on Wednesday.

She told Siobhan that she was going to say goodbye to Father McQuarters at St. Agnes on Tuesday. Her cousin wanted to go with her, but Ingrid insisted on going by herself. She would take the bus to and from the parish one last time. She would gaze out at the storefronts and homes that held so many memories for her. Ingrid would pass the site where Cullan was killed and the cemetery where he and Richard Brennan were buried. She would tend the flowers in the parish garden one last time. Siobhan protested, but she understood.

This visit with the priest was something Ingrid needed to do alone.

CHAPTER TWENTY-SIX

Ingrid was about to knock on the door of the residence behind St. Agnes' Parish, but Father McQuarters was just walking out as she arrived. He was wearing his gardening outfit and that made her grin, but it hurt her face to smile.

"May I offer you a cup of tea?" he asked. "I still have this day to put you to work with the flowers. They have missed you."

"I've missed them, Father," replied Ingrid. "I've missed you, too. I'm going to miss you."

"That's the sweetest thing anyone has said to me lately," he said. "Too many funerals in a row."

"I know," said Ingrid. "I was there."

They walked into the residence together. The apartment was sparsely furnished, but comfortable. Father McQuarters liked to paint. His canvases were all over the room. Most of his paintings were unfinished. Ingrid sat at the kitchen table as he prepared their tea service.

"Milk? Honey? Cream?" he asked.

"All!" answered Ingrid. "The truth is, Father, that I don't like tea very much."

"It's an acquired taste," he answered. "Just like the truth."

This was a dance usually reserved for adults. It was no accident that Ingrid wanted to see Father McQuarters alone and it was no accident that he had cleared his afternoon schedule to visit with her. It was like they were two balloons being overfilled with water and unsure of which would be first to burst.

"Do you remember much from Thursday night?" asked the priest.

"Too much," said Ingrid.

"Would you prefer we spoke about these matters in the confessional booth?" he asked. "You might be more comfortable there."

"No," she answered. "This is fine. I like your paintings."

"Thank you," he said.

Ingrid seized the opportunity to take control of the conversation. Her maturity was blossoming like the flowers in the garden outside his door.

"I saw you talk to those men at the pub at my party, Father," said Ingrid. "When you weren't dancing. One of them came to see me at the hospital."

"You're a very observant young lady, Ingrid," he replied. "What was said at this visit?"

Father McQuarters had not bothered to ask what men she was referring to at the pub that night. They both knew the answer.

"He wanted to know if I remembered anything in particular."

"Did you?" asked the priest.

"Yes," she said.

"Did you tell him?"

Ingrid paused.

"No, I didn't tell him anything. I want to tell you."

"Then tell me, my child," said Father McQuarters.

"My cousin Ciaran was one of the people attacking Paddy," cried Ingrid. "He had a hood on but I know it was him."

"Are you sure of this?" he asked

"Yes."

"But how can you be completely sure of this?" said the priest. "You were obviously disoriented and distracted. You had been hit and kicked. There was a lot of tumult. How can you be sure?"

"I'm sure, Father." said Ingrid. "I have proof."

"And what is this proof, my girl?"

"I saw Ciaran's red socks," she replied. "He always wears red socks under his combat boots. I know it was him."

"A lot of people wear red socks," said Father McQuarters. "I wear red socks sometimes. Paddy is missing and you've been through a horrible ordeal. We can't make an allegation based on the color of someone's socks."

"I didn't tell the police about this," Ingrid continued. "I didn't tell my family. I didn't tell the man from the pub who visited me in the hospital. I'm telling you."

"We need more proof, dear," he whispered.

"I have it."

Ingrid stood and walked to the couch by the door to the residence. She had set her purse upon it after entering the room.

"Here," she said. "I have the proof here."

Ingrid reached into her purse and pulled out the note that Ciaran had written for Paddy. She handed it to Father McQuarters.

"Ciaran gave me that on Thursday," said Ingrid, her voice choking with emotion. "I gave it to Paddy to read later that day, Father. Now, he's gone and he's not coming back."

Father McQuarters sat back in his chair. He held the note in both hands and read it several times, then stood and removed his glasses. He paced the room. Ingrid watched him as his facial expression went through several changes.

After a few moments, he sat down again, put on his glasses, and looked at the note once more.

"You're a brave young woman," said the priest. "An extremely brave young woman. Does anyone else know about this note?"

"No one, Father," said Ingrid. "Just us."

"Does anyone else know about you seeing Ciaran's red socks?"

"No one, Father," she repeated. "Just us."

Father McQuarters took off his glasses once more. He was visibly shaken now. It was the first time Ingrid had seen him in less than jovial spirits other than at the funerals he had officiated.

"We should not speak of this again, okay?" he asked.

"I promise," said Ingrid. "I don't want to talk about any of this ever again."

"May I keep the note?"

"Yes, Father," she said. "Keep it. Do whatever you need to with it."

Father McQuarters raised his eyebrows and looked directly into Ingrid's eyes. She looked back at him without blinking. Ingrid sensed that he understood both the fragility she was trying to mask and the impending, further doom for the community.

"You're a brave young woman," he said again. "I'm going to miss you."

They spent an hour in the garden together watering flowers and repotting a few plants that had outgrown their original homes. Not a word was spoken. Father McQuarters moved one of his stereo speakers to the window of his residence so they could listen to classical music. This was one aspect of Belfast that Ingrid was going to miss. She contemplated what he was going to do with the information she had provided about Ciaran.

"I have to go," she said. "I am going to miss you, Father. I hope we can still be pen pals."

"You'll never be forgotten, dear Ingrid," he answered. "I can promise you that. Belfast needs a few more like you."

He walked Ingrid to the stop across the street and waited there with her until a bus arrived. Too much had been said to engage in small talk. Ingrid hugged him goodbye and gave him a peck on the cheek like a teenage girl would to her grandfather. She boarded the bus and waved to him. Father McQuarters waved back with his free hand.

His other hand was in the front left pocket of his pants clutching Ciaran's note.

CHAPTER TWENTY-SEVEN

The car ride to Belfast International Airport with Niall, Mary, and Siobhan was silent. Too many tears had been shed and too many hearts had been broken since Ingrid's arrival in May to reminisce about her visit. There had been no word of Paddy's whereabouts from the RUC. He was presumed to have been interrogated and murdered by one of the loyalist factions running amok in Northern Ireland. Assigning exact blame was useless at this point. Nothing could be done to bring Paddy back. Ingrid knew who was most responsible.

Her parents had arranged for a return flight from Belfast instead of Dublin, but this meant an extra connection for Ingrid. She would fly to London, then to Dallas, and finally to Shreveport.

August 5 was an ominous day to leave the island. The IRA detonated a series of explosives in seven areas of Northern Ireland that included Belfast, Derry, and Lisburn. These attacks came on the heels of two RUC officers being killed by an IRA mine in County Tyrone just two days earlier. It appeared the Provos were running amok, too.

Ingrid stared out the window at a plane taking off in the distance. She wished that she were on it and not about to wait several hours for her own flight. Her thoughts were drifting back to the anticipation and excitement she felt leaving Shreveport at the start of her journey. Now, beaten and bruised, she felt like a failure. It was the first time in her life that she had experienced loss other than having her family's first dog pass away when she was in kindergarten. Ingrid thought about Laura losing her father. At the time, she was not able to process her friend's feelings. She understood now.

Niall carried her suitcase into the terminal while Mary and Siobhan walked on each side of Ingrid and held her hands. She was wearing the birthday sweater. The cards, letters, and notes from Paddy and Moira were in her purse. Tears were in her eyes. Ingrid was still a bit groggy, but her mind was clear enough to realize that going home early was the best choice for everyone.

She did not want to be in Belfast another second.

The hugs and kisses goodbye at the security checkpoint were strained. Niall's face had aged in the short time since Cullan's death, as had Mary's, and Siobhan's joyful exuberance had turned into bitterness. They embraced together as a family and Ingrid began to weep. There were simply no words that could be said to mollify her feelings of depression and disappointment.

Niall, Mary, and Siobhan watched Ingrid walk to her departure gate. Perhaps, for a moment, they hoped she would turn back to wave or smile. She did not. She was too numb to feel any sense of familial obligation at the airport. Ingrid simply wanted to get on her plane as soon as possible and get moving.

She thought about what happened to Declan. That should have been a red flag. That should have been a warning sign. Ingrid was not equipped at the time to see it as an omen portending doom.

Her life had not come full circle since then; it had been shifted in an opposing direction.

This was a different Ingrid. She had wanted to be new and improved at sixteen. Instead, she felt the weight of the world upon her shoulders. Carefree days at one of the lakes near Shreveport wearing a new bathing suit for the first time before the school year began would not erase what she had seen and experienced.

Over the Atlantic Ocean again, Ingrid opened her diary and started writing. She would not stop for several hours. The flight attendants had to bring her several additional pens because she kept running out of ink. Ingrid was in a frenzy. She was bleeding onto the pages: her blood, Cullan's, Paddy's. She thought about the editorials she had written for the student newspaper at St. Vincent's Academy and how immaterial the subject matter for each had been. How could she be concerned about dress codes and bell schedules now? It disgusted her to think that she had been afraid to attach her name to these offerings. There was a world out there beyond Saddle Oxford shoes and light blue button-down shirts.

From this moment forward, Ingrid resolved, she would never do anything anonymously.

She made additional resolutions, too. Ingrid was going to protect her sister. She was not going to sit idly by in classes at school and let others be bullied. No matter where she was on the planet, Ingrid was not going to turn her back and walk away from Niall, Mary, and Siobhan again. She took a break from her diary and wrote them a note of thanks.

The words from Father McQuarters rang in her ears. *You're a brave young woman*. She did not want to let him down.

Ingrid closed her diary and her eyes. There were a few hours remaining in the flight to Dallas. She needed sleep, but that was impossible. She kept thinking about Paddy. Why did it all have to be so perfect and so sad at the same time? Ingrid could smell his clothing. She could taste the champagne they shared at the botanical gardens. She could feel his fingers running through her hair and his breathing upon her neck.

How could any of her friends at SVA relate to having their first love dragged away to his death? Ingrid thought of Mrs. Morton's summer assignment. She wished many of her adventures had been fiction.

The summer in Belfast felt like an inescapable blur. Ingrid needed to see the benefit from it. There were moments when she felt that she wanted to give up and quit. What did that mean? Seamus and Kathleen had not raised a quitter. An image popped into her head of the plane crashing so that she could die and join Paddy and Cullan in heaven, but then she thought of how ridiculous that sounded. The rest of the passengers did not need to suffer because she was heartbroken.

Ingrid thought of the many runs she had shared with her father and how all of her training in Belfast had been when she was alone. Those moments with Seamus always seemed to clear her mind from worries, doubts, and fears. Ingrid reflected upon them. Color came back to her face. She could feel it. Then a chill came over her body. It was not the product of fear. It was anticipatory strength. Her flight was going to be landing shortly, but Ingrid had made the decision to soar. It had taken more than ten hours of travel high above the clouds to figure it out.

Yes, she was filled with questions and self-doubt. Yes, the only two places she had lived during her lifetime—Shreveport and Belfast—were diametrically opposed to one another. And, yes, her cousin and boyfriend were both dead. Ingrid was 16 and the choice was up to her: she could live the rest of the life as a hermit or she could push herself to flourish. Giving up would have been to choose the former.

The latter is what she would choose. She resigned herself to that decision.

Through all of these deliberations, Ingrid had not noticed how firmly her hands were gripping the legs of her jeans. Her knuckles had turned white, just like when she and Siobhan had held each other after their border crossing experience into Northern Ireland, and she felt perspiration in her palms. This was a good sign. Ingrid felt less medicated than the past several days. These were her body's true reactions. She did not like the way she felt on the painkillers or after the sedatives had worn out their effectiveness. She knew they were, initially, necessary considering her condition at the time, but now she felt more like herself.

The new self. The new Ingrid. She would retain her sensitivities and her thirst for knowledge, but she would be stronger—mentally and physically—-and fearless. *I am empowering myself. I am never going to quit.* She felt chills again. Girls of her age in Shreveport did not think this way. Ingrid did now.

She thought how her parents might expect her to land in Shreveport as a whimpering child because of all that had transpired in Belfast. They were about to discover the brave young woman she had become and so was everyone else there. Ingrid went through customs in Dallas and had a two-hour wait for the short flight to Shreveport. She loved and missed her parents, but her mind was on Moira. Whatever happened to her sister at the lake house with Clooney was the final injustice of the summer.

Ingrid had never told anyone her secret. She had locked it so far away in the recesses of her mind for so long that it was more of an annoyance to her when she thought about it, instead of being the most traumatic event of her life prior to Belfast. Now, she regretted never telling her parents. They would have believed her. They could have protected Moira. By telling them, she could have saved her sister. Ingrid felt a rush of sorrow overcome her as she looked out over the horizon from the terminal in Texas. The sky was a mixture of orange, yellow, and red colors as the sun began to set in the distance. This panorama seemed to capture Ingrid's despondency about what had happened to her with Clooney and what had just happened to her sister.

Ingrid remembered how it felt to have her uncle's hands on her body. The incident had not lasted more than a few seconds before she was able to break free from his grip and hide in the woods until he passed out into another one of his drunken naps. Still, it had occurred. She had come back from the dock after trying to catch fish with a bamboo pole, rusty hook, and some dead worms. Clooney had been drinking all day. Her parents were at a wedding and, instead of going with them, she had chosen to go swimming under the care of her father's brother. She had always blamed herself for making that decision. Ingrid beat herself up over it.

She imagined Moira escaping to safety like she had done. Ingrid prayed that was the case. She wanted her sister to be a *brave young woman*, too. Ingrid thought about what had happened with Ciaran on the night that Cullan was killed. She shuddered at the thought of him doing that to Siobhan. Ciaran unwittingly led his own brother to be killed by a car bomb, set up Ingrid's boyfriend—his good friend—for death, and now had a history of trying to fondle two female members of his own family. Ingrid remembered her Greek grandmother on her mother's side saying that some people, like cars, were just lemons. Clooney and Ciaran were lemons.

Paddy was not a lemon, nor was Cullan. Fergal, Jimmy, and Eddie were not lemons, either. Ingrid reasoned that the older and wiser she got, the better she would be able to read people and their intentions.

An announcement came over the terminal loudspeaker that her flight to Shreveport would be boarding soon. It was just a short hop from Dallas by air and a three-hour drive in a car. Three hours was the duration of the bus ride from Dublin to Belfast.

As she walked down the ramp to the plane, Ingrid felt the stifling heat and humidity of an August afternoon in Texas. It was a world away from the feeling she first had in Ireland.

CHAPTER TWENTY-EIGHT

Moira sprinted to Ingrid and hugged her around the waist. Seamus and Kathleen arrived moments later and embraced their daughters together. The scene drew scant attention from the tired crowd deplaning into the terminal at Shreveport Regional Airport. To Ingrid, Moira's grip felt like she was holding on for dear life. That was fine. Her sister could hold her and hug her for as long as she wanted.

Ingrid looked into the misty eyes of her parents. They were glowing with radiant smiles, but they also gave off nervous signs of stress and fear. She hugged and kissed them. She kissed Moira's cheeks and the top of her head. Ingrid felt that stepping out of this moment would be awkward. The small talk as they walked together to the car in the parking lot proved this to be true.

It did not matter how her flights were. It did not matter if she was hungry or not. It did not matter if she was tired. Ingrid knew those questions were coming, but she did not feel like answering them. She wanted to be alone with her sister. She wanted to hear Moira tell her what had happened with Clooney at the lake house.

Seamus went the fastest way home from the airport by taking I-20 East onto Line Avenue and heading south. They would arrive in less than ten minutes. Ingrid gazed to her right as they passed Jordan Street to see the main building for Jesuit High School. She thought of her friends there and wondered if she would see them before school started. A few blocks later she looked left to see Byrd High

School. Ingrid enjoyed running on the track behind the school with her father. He had taught her how to do interval training and it had really improved her pace.

Ingrid loved South Highlands. The oak trees and the old homes were so flavorful. Each yard was impeccably maintained. All of the memories of her life were here. She thought of Laura and what their reunion would be like the following day. She thought of what the cliques were doing. Was Becky pregnant? Was Cami in jail? Ingrid wondered if she would be able to complete Mrs. Morton's assignment in the next two weeks. She wanted to play games with her sister and bake cookies with her mom.

She had memories of her life in Belfast, too. Ingrid worried that they would turn into nightmares. The trauma of what had occurred in such a short amount of time filled her with antipathy for recollecting it all. Ingrid wanted to block out all of the bad and only reflect on the good, but the two conflicting sides were as interwoven as the wool strands of her new Aran sweater. She longed for the simple life that Shreveport could provide in the last two weeks of her summer break.

Laura had constructed an enormous sign welcoming Ingrid home and left it on the doorstep for her best friend to find. Ingrid was too tired to smile, but she did. Entering the house was surreal for her. Ingrid had not slept in her own bed since May and had not slept alone in a bed since the night before Ciaran's attack. She missed the comfy assortment of pillows and stuffed animals. One was always within her reach to hug. She had also missed one of her favorite weekly rituals: taking a bubble bath on Sunday nights. Niall and Mary's home in Belfast only had showers, so the notion of soaking in a tub, reading *National Geographic*, and listening to The Beatles again gave her a measure of peace. There was homemade banana bread and vanilla ice cream waiting for her. Ingrid did not feel like eating. It was good to be home, but she was exhausted and excused herself to her room instead of chatting with her parents and sister in the kitchen. She just wanted to fall asleep as soon as possible and then wake up in the morning as if nothing at all had happened in Northern Ireland.

It was now morning on Thursday, August 6. Ingrid was asleep in her bed with the right side of her head on a pillow and her left arm around a giant teddy bear. Its name was Charlie and had been given to her by Moira at Christmas several years ago. Charlie was her go-to snuggle buddy. She had slept through the night, but suddenly felt the warmth of a hand upon her left shoulder. Ingrid sat up hurriedly and screamed.

"No!" she yelled. "No!"

Laura jerked her body back and got off of the bed.

"Ingrid! Ingrid! It's me. It's Laura!"

Ingrid looked around the room and recognized where she was, then shook her head and fell back onto her pillows.

"I'm sorry for startling you," said Laura. "I just wanted to surprise you and see you as soon as I could."

"I'm sorry," answered Ingrid. "I'm glad it was you."

Laura got back onto the bed and gave Ingrid a hug. The two rolled around frolicking and laughing as they had always done. Pillows and stuffed animals were sent careening over the sides of the bed onto the floor.

"I have so much to tell you," said Ingrid.

"I know," replied Laura. "You can whenever you're ready. No rush. We have the rest of our lives."

"What's been going on in Shreveport?" asked Ingrid.

"Here?" answered Laura. "What do you think? Nothing, of course. No gossip, no scandals. I had one date with Aaron Kerouac. We went to a movie at the mall, ate popcorn, then his car got a flat tire and his dad had to pick us up. Great date!"

"Did you kiss him?"

"Nope," said Laura. "He tried to hold my hand during the movie, but I told him I had a rash."

With that, the best friends began giggling and wrestling around again. Their physical contact seemed to reacquaint the emotional bond that had been put on hold by Ingrid's journey. The girls collapsed next to one another and stared up at the ceiling to watch the fan there spin around and around.

"I was really worried about you," said Laura.

"I know," replied Ingrid. "Thank you. I was worried about me, too."

The door to Ingrid's room had been left ajar by Laura, so neither of them heard Moira come in until she leapt upon the bed and landed between them.

"Oh, Bug," said Ingrid. "I am so happy to see you again."

"I missed you more than Laura did," answered Moira.

"No, you didn't," said Laura.

"Yes, I did."

"Didn't," replied Laura.

"Did," said Moira.

"You two! Stop!" chortled Ingrid. "Who is making me breakfast on my first day back? That's the important question."

The three girls lumbered downstairs to the kitchen. Kathleen had prepared a feast for the family. Too much food, really, and Ingrid looked upon the spread as she had the plates and containers people in Lower Falls delivered to Niall and Mary after Cullan was killed.

She paused. It was her first breakfast back at home with her family and she had already made a reference in her mind to an event in Belfast. These thoughts will pass in time, she reasoned. There were so many other things to focus upon before going back to St. Vincent's Academy.

Seamus came into the house and joined the party around the table. He sat down next to Ingrid and gave her a kiss on the cheek. Her father was such a good man, thought Ingrid, just like Niall. She was so excited to start running with him again. Being at home with her family and best friend made Ingrid feel that this moment was the first step of her recovery. It was odd for her, however, to possess the knowledge that she had changed so much and that no one else here knew about it. Her outward appearance to them was the same, except for the cuts and bruises that remained, but she was a different person on the inside. Ingrid wanted them to know that she was a *brave young woman* now. She wondered how she would go about proving it.

Moira was acting normal to her in these initial reunion moments. Ingrid did not sense the same disillusionment she had felt after her own incident with Clooney. Her sister was smiling and laughing, which was much better than how her mother had described her on the phone, and was interacting in a healthy manner. Hearing that Moira had been withdrawn, quiet, and pensive had made Ingrid shudder with fright. She knew those feelings. She knew what it meant to impose limitations on one's own expressiveness as a defense mechanism.

After breakfast, Ingrid and Laura went upstairs again. They were now faced with the same dilemma that every Shreveport teenager was experiencing at the same time: what to do today. There were only so many summer jobs to go around and, since Ingrid had been gone for so long, the chances of her getting one for the two weeks before classes at SVA resumed were not good. Laura was a babysitter for several families and had made some decent money. Ingrid had babysitting jobs during the school year, too. Word had spread among young mothers that they were two of the most responsible girls in South Highlands, so the duo capitalized.

Ingrid and Laura each had their driver's licenses, but no cars. They had friends with cars, but coordinating activities with teenagers spread out across Shreveport was not always easy. Riding the local bus was unacceptable. The thought of being seen on one was horrific to them. Laura was fascinated when Ingrid told her that she rode the bus to and from St. Agnes' Parish almost every day. The girls decided that taking it easy at Ingrid's house would be their best option today. They could catch up, play board games, do art projects, and hang out with Moira. Laura's mom worked full-time as a paralegal at a downtown law firm, so most if not all of her time away from home on weekdays was spent at the Fallon's home.

Even though there seemed to be an immediate return to summer normalcy, Ingrid was stressed. She felt that she had so many things to do and just a short time in which to do them. It was evening in Belfast, six hours ahead of Louisiana time, and she knew her body's clock would take a few more days to adjust itself to this time zone. Her room looked the same. The house looked the same. Moira was a hair taller and Laura seemed to be even more fit. Her parents never changed. They looked great to her. Ingrid was trying to process it all. She felt that the environment was like a Hollywood set and that a director was about to yell "Cut!" It did not seem real to her.

As she helped Laura and Moira with a massive jigsaw puzzle on the living room floor, Ingrid thought of Paddy. It was exactly one week ago to the day he was abducted. She did not want to look at the clock on the wall at 3:00 p.m. That would be too painful. She thought about her bike ride in the rain to the meeting spot by Linfield FC's stadium. It had been a nightmare.

Ingrid caught Moira looking at her and smiled. It was another sunny, humid day in Shreveport. Oak trees provided shade for the front of her house and pine trees did the same in the back. The Fallons rarely turned on their air conditioner units during the summer. Each room had at least one fan. The girls continued with their puzzle. Ingrid realized that she had not yet checked on her Irish lilies. She thought of Father McQuarters—both his gardening lessons and their last conversation—and wondered whether she would ever see him again.

Her mind was racing and she could not seem to calm down. It was anxiety, the type brought on my both anticipation and lament, and Ingrid was having trouble processing the transition from Belfast to Shreveport.

The world within her had changed.

CHAPTER TWENTY-NINE

Ingrid had been back in Shreveport for five days. She had not yet written a letter to her family in Belfast or to Father McQuarters. Over the weekend, while she spent time with Laura and Moira rearranging her bedroom furniture and painting the walls a shade of pastel green, Thomas McElwee became the ninth hunger striker to die. There were riots and murders all across Northern Ireland, too. The most excitement for Ingrid and Laura was running into Team CCM at Mall St. Vincent.

The girls had walked along Fairfield Avenue, past Betty Virginia Park on their right, and made a left onto Ratcliff Street into the mall's parking lot. It was their regular route to SVA and they were thrilled to see the new action movie with Harrison Ford that people were talking about called *Raiders of the Lost Ark.* Ingrid and Laura were also thrilled to see Cami, Carole, and Meredith there. How could they not be? The trio were as entertaining as any summer blockbuster.

Mall St. Vincent had a particular pecking order for local teenagers. Geeky boys with braces and zits wasted their weekly allowances on video games at the arcade. Sophisticated juniors and seniors on dates dined on Mexican food at El Chico. Everyone, however, went to the movies and walked laps around the mall's single floor to check out everyone else.

Laura spotted Team CCM first. They were standing in front of the theater entrance making obscene gestures with corn dogs. This act quickly degenerated into Meredith splattering mustard on Carole's face. The two began a playful slap fight with corn dogs and other condiments until Cami finally restored order.

"Ladies," she implored. "Not in public!"

A group of shoppers on a Monday outing took a wide path around Team CCM's mayhem.

"Hope to not be you someday," sneered Cami to the women. "Looks like a lot of fun."

Ingrid and Laura got into a short line to buy their tickets for the movie. They did not expect anyone to notice them.

"Ingrid Fallon," barked Cami. "Hi!"

Ingrid was not sure if she was hearing things or not at first and thought her concussion had returned.

"Ingrid!" repeated Cami. "How's your summer?"

Laura looked at Ingrid and raised her eyebrows. They both were caught off-guard by the greeting.

"I just got back," said Ingrid. "I went to visit family for two months."

"In Northern Ireland, right?" asked Cami.

Laura turned to Ingrid and raised her eyebrows again.

"Yes," answered Ingrid.

"Well, I hope to hear all about it. I doubt I'll ever get over there, but one never knows."

Carole and Meredith stood behind Cami wiping mustard off of their faces. They smiled and nodded at Ingrid and Laura.

"What movie are you seeing?" asked Cami.

"*Raiders of the Lost Ark*," answered Laura. "What are you guys seeing?"

"I want to see *Endless Love*," said Carole. "But these bitches want to see your movie, too."

"We are all going to *Raiders of the Lost Ark*," said Cami. "And that's final."

Soon, the five classmates from St. Vincent's Academy were seated in the same row of a movie theater together at Mall St. Vincent. Ingrid remembered how Cami used to ridicule anyone who even thought of going to this mall. Now, here she was, sitting next to the leader of Team CCM as Indiana Jones battled Nazis. The girls chomped on the popcorn and chocolate that was passed between them.

"What you want to do is to put some chocolate in your mouth and suck on it until it melts, then put some popcorn in your mouth and eat it together," advised Cami. "Delicious!"

"You just want something in your mouth to suck on," said Meredith.

All of the girls laughed. Laura, sitting in the aisle seat to Ingrid's left, softly elbowed her best friend in the ribs. They would *never* speak to one another like that.

Ingrid felt a strange kinship with Cami. She did not know her very well, but she was intrigued at how someone so blatantly wild could also be one of her rivals for top marks at SVA. Cami had an attitude about her that was brazen and confident. That spirit reminded her of Siobhan at the start of the summer.

"I have something to ask you," whispered Ingrid into Cami's ear.

"Ask me anything you want," answered Cami.

"Do you ever think about what happened with Becky and Celeste in Mrs. Morton's class?"

"Yes," said Cami. "All the time."

"Me, too," replied Ingrid.

"I'm kind of obsessed with it, actually," said Cami. "The *dumb black bitch* thing has to be responded to, but who's going to do it?"

Cami winked at her. Ingrid nodded her head and looked at the screen. She had a new and profound sense of respect for Team CCM's leader. Ingrid felt like Cami was the only person in Shreveport to recognize the changes inside of her. And they had only spoken a few words to one another!

After the movie, the five girls walked out of the mall into the oppressive humidity of Louisiana.

"There she is," said Cami, pointing at St. Vincent's Academy across the parking lot.

"Two more weeks of freedom!" shouted Meredith. "Save us!"

Carole put her hand on Ingrid's shoulder.

"Where did you park?" asked Carole.

"We walked," answered Laura.

"Not today," said Carole. "We'll give you a ride."

Laura looked at Ingrid and they both grinned. Carole had a red Jeep, the top was down, and the ride would save them from sweating profusely on the walk up Fairfield Avenue. The girls piled into the vehicle—Cami rode shotgun—and soon a Van Halen song was blasting from the speakers. Laura looked at Ingrid again when Carole made a left onto Ratcliff Street instead of a right. She had to lean forward to do so because Meredith sat between them on the back bench seat.

"We live by South Highlands Elementary," yelled Ingrid over David Lee Roth's vocals.

Cami looked over her left shoulder to face the passengers in the back.

"I know where you live," she screamed. "But Carole doesn't."

"Yeah," yelled Carole. "And I said I was giving you a ride, not a ride home."

Ingrid and Laura expressed a combination of puzzlement and joy on their faces. They felt *cool*. Ingrid sensed her hair flying everywhere in the wind as Carole sped along East Kings Highway past Centenary College on the left, where Seamus taught, and the pies at Strawn's on the right. She had not had wind in her face like this since being aboard Paddy's motorcycle that last time.

Carole Evans did not have a problem running red lights. This was clear to all in the Jeep because she ran three of them before they got to the Red River.

"Are we going to Bossier City?" asked Ingrid.

"Never!" yelled Cami.

Just before the bridge that leads across to Barksdale Air Force Base, Carole made a sharp right turn off of the road into a field of loose dirt. She did not slow down, either, and the three girls in the back had to grab the roll bars to avoid flying out of the Jeep. They drove in and out of marshy terrain until they entered a clearing along the clay-colored banks of the river. Ingrid was not sure how close they were to Hamel's Amusement Park, one of Shreveport's few attractions other than the horse track called Louisiana Downs, but it seemed like they could smell the cotton candy there.

"Time for beer," exclaimed Meredith while climbing over the backside of the Jeep.

She pulled a cooler from behind the bench seat and opened it to reveal six bottles of Coors.

"Time for a tan," said Cami.

Ingrid and Laura stood next to one another as Cami took off her shirt and shorts. Carole did, too, then Meredith as well. It was strange to witness the sense of freedom that the three members of Team CCM exhibited. Ingrid and Laura were fully-clothed while Cami, Carole, and Meredith stood in their bras and underwear holding bottles of beer.

"You're making us uncomfortable," said Cami. "Take off your clothes."

"This isn't one of those tricks where you leave us here in our underwear, is it?" asked Laura.

"We wouldn't be sharing our beer with you if it was," said Meredith, handing bottles to Ingrid and Laura.

The best friends took sips of their beers as they removed their shirts and shorts. When girls changed clothes for gym class at SVA, it was done so secretly and modestly between lockers that no one dared look around at anyone else. Being at a pool or the lake in a bathing suit was one thing, but this was something else entirely.

"That's better," said Carole. "Now we can trust you."

As the sounds of Van Halen's first album continued to blare over the Jeep's speakers, the five high school juniors-to-be stood in their underwear drinking beer while looking out at the muddy, slow-moving Red River. Team CCM lit cigarettes and blew perfect smoke rings. Across the water, two old fisherman stared at the girls in dumbfounded wonderment.

"Is this what you do all of the time?" asked Ingrid.

"This is about it," answered Cami. "What do you think we do? Rob liquor stores?"

"Yes," said Laura.

"Well, that's funny," replied Cami. "The girls everyone thinks are so good at our school are actually the bad ones. And vice versa."

"I'll drink to that!" shouted Carole.

And that is how most of the afternoon of August 10 went for Ingrid Fallon and Laura Wheeler with new best-friends-forever Cami McMillan, Carole Evans, and Meredith Tyler.

Carole got Ingrid and Laura back home in time for dinner. When she pulled in front of Ingrid's house, the sun was almost over the horizon. Its last rays of light shone through the shade trees lining Erie Street. Shreveport could possess ethereal beauty at times. One just had to find it. The girls all smelled like beer and cigarettes when they left the river, but the fresh air of the car ride and a few sticks of gum cured that issue.

"We should do this again," said Cami. "It was fun."

"I would like that," answered Ingrid.

"Me, too," said Laura.

Ingrid and Laura waved goodbye and Team CCM roared onto Line Avenue with the Jeep's tires squealing. The girls sat down on the porch steps and looked across at the elementary school field. Seamus and Moira were there playing soccer together. Ingrid thought about the soccer boys in Belfast and seeing Paddy for the first time. His fluidity stuck in her mind. He had the same body movements when they were slow dancing together by the fountain at the botanical gardens. She could not believe that he had disappeared in front of her eyes.

Laura looked at Ingrid and sensed her sadness.

"Do you want to talk about it?" she asked. "No rush. No pressure from me. When you're ready, you're ready."

"I'm not sure I'll ever be able to talk about it," said Ingrid. "But, when I am, it will be with you."

"That makes me happy," replied Laura.

"I can tell you this," said Ingrid. "It's not the streets you live on that matter in life, but what you do on those streets."

Laura grabbed Ingrid's hand and squeezed it.

"Don't worry," said Laura. "I don't have a rash."

The girls giggled together. It was one of those teenage bonding moments that ensures a future together of sharing secrets and unlocking each other's souls. Laura would always be there for Ingrid as a confidant and sounding board. She was not judgmental. Instead, she was a good listener who placed her friend's happiness above her own.

They went into the house and smelled a crock-pot full of brisket, potatoes, carrots, onions, and spices. Kathleen pulled fresh biscuits out of the oven and smiled as Ingrid and Laura sat down at the kitchen table. Moira ran into the room and grabbed a biscuit.

"I'm starving!" she said.

"Please save room for supper," said Kathleen. "I'm glad to see your appetite is back."

Ingrid watched her sister douse the snack with butter and honey. Moira seemed so innocent and pure, just as Ingrid had felt arriving in Dublin. That changed for her with Declan's beating. It changed with every calamitous event in Belfast. She wanted to approach her sister about what had happened with Clooney at the lake house, but now was not the time.

Seamus entered the kitchen and put his arms around Kathleen. They were never shy about displaying their affection for one another in public. It was a level of comfort that Ingrid admired. It was one she had felt with Paddy. Ingrid wondered if she would ever feel that way again.

CHAPTER THIRTY

Ingrid got in several good runs with her father around their neighborhood before her junior year at SVA began. Each time, Seamus would press for a bit more information about Belfast. She knew that he had been communicating with Niall and Mary about all that had transpired there and she appreciated his concern, but she did not go into anything more than peripheral details. Ingrid did not want her father to know about the sexual assault at the hands of the British soldiers or Ciaran. She did not want him to know what it felt like to watch Paddy be dragged away to his death. Ingrid did not want to lie to her father, but she did not want to tell him the entire truth, either.

Their workouts always began as slow jogs and evolved into furious sprints. This is the way they evolved historically and seemed to be the product of the competitive spirit that their father-daughter rivalry got flowing. Seamus told Ingrid that her stamina and strength would increase if she pushed herself harder at the end of their runs when she was most fatigued. She needed this motivation from her father. After all of her physical trauma, she wanted to build herself up as strong as possible before the start of the new semester at SVA. At least that is the reason she gave to her parents.

They went for a solemn jog together on the Friday before school started. On the previous day, August 20, Michael Devine passed away in Northern Ireland. He was 27 and the last of the ten men do die on hunger strikes at

Maze Prison. Ingrid's summer had begun with the death of Bobby Sands and now it was ending in similar fashion. She made a vow to plant lilies in her backyard for all of the hunger strikers and tend to the flowers with the same compassion she showed the ones dedicated to Cullan and Paddy.

"May I borrow the station wagon next Sunday morning?" asked Ingrid as they turned the corner onto Erie Street from Fairfield Avenue for the final stretch home.

"Sure," answered Seamus. "You're planning ahead!"

"I need to help Cami with some errands," said Ingrid.

"No problem," said her father. "You have your license so you're good to go."

When she got home, Ingrid asked Moira if she would like to have a picnic on Saturday. Her younger sister, of course, accepted the invitation. There were two days remaining in their summer vacation. Moira would be entering the seventh grade at Agnew and was excited for all of the new clothes she was going to wear. The majority of those outfits were hand-me-downs from Ingrid, but they all felt like Cinderella's gown to her. The sisters walked on Line Avenue to Betty Virginia Park at the bottom of the hill and found an open table. Ingrid had gone all out: there was a red gingham tablecloth with matching napkins, cold cuts, cheese, sourdough bread, pickles, spicy mustard, mayonnaise, and soda. Kathleen had helped stock the family's wicker picnic basket with Ingrid and had even snuck in some homemade sugar cookies for a dessert surprise.

"I love you, Bug," said Ingrid. "I really do."

"I know," answered Moira.

"It's so good to be back home with everyone. I missed you most of all."

"I missed you, too," said Moira. "I wish you had never left."

"Sometimes I feel the same way, Bug," replied Ingrid.

She paused to gather her composure and thought how much she wished this conversation would have been one she had with her mother several years ago.

"I need to know what happened at the lake house with Uncle Clooney," said Ingrid.

Moira looked deeply into her older sister's eyes.

"He tried to touch me," said Moira. "I wouldn't let him, but he kept trying."

"Where?" asked Ingrid, her lips tightening. "Where did he try to touch you?"

"Everywhere," answered Moira. "And he tried to kiss me."

Ingrid could feel the blood boiling as it ran through her heart. She also felt a chill down her spine. Her fists clenched and her knuckles turned white.

"Did you get away from him?" asked Ingrid.

"Yes," said Moira. "He started chasing me around the house and fell down and hit his head. I hid on the houseboat until Daddy came to pick me up. No one would ever look there."

"Smart girl," said Ingrid. "You are a smart girl."

It took all of her poise and grace to remain calm and emotionless in front of her scared little sister.

"It wasn't your fault," continued Ingrid. "It was not your fault."

"I don't want to go back to the lake house," said Moira.

"You never have to go back there again," replied Ingrid. "I promise."

The girls finished their picnic and walked home. Moira picked flowers along the way and gave them to her mother. It seemed, to Ingrid, that Moira had avoided a fate that could have been much worse. She was grateful and relieved, but she still harbored guilt for remaining silent about Clooney's previous attempt to touch her. That would have made a difference. Moira might never have been in that situation. Though she had not said a prayer since assisting Father McQuarters at Richard Brennan's funeral, Ingrid said one in her head and asked for the strength to be a *brave young woman*. Her opportunity to do so would come in the first week of school.

There was a frenetic energy in the hallways of St. Vincent's Academy. Ninth grade students wandered around trying to figure out where their classes were, new teachers tried to win over their classrooms, and the two ruling cliques had to once again establish their territories for hangout spots at breaks and lunch. It was Tuesday, August 25. Ingrid and Laura stood chatting next to their lockers. Junior year would be incredibly tougher than when they were sophomores: each would be in an honors track curriculum with Mrs. Morton's English III possibly their most arduous test. The girls were nervous, but also eagerly anticipating the challenge ahead. Becky Harken, Cami McMillan, and Celeste Wilson would be in Honors English III with them. The rest of the clique members would not.

When Ingrid and Laura entered Mrs. Morton's first class of the school year, they were surprised to see Cami already there saving two seats for them.

"We're all sitting together," she said. "And that's the way it's going to be."

Laura smiled and Ingrid shook her head with pleasure. Their day at the river with Team CCM had elevated the pair into a new social strata. This was not lost on Becky Harken who, as she set her belongings down next to her desk on the other side of the room, glared at Cami.

"I'm going to have to do something about that troll," said Cami.

"I'll handle it," said Ingrid.

Cami and Laura looked at one another quizzically. They had never heard Ingrid make a threatening comment before.

Mrs. Morton entered the room and, as the bell rang to begin the period, Celeste did the late-for-class fast walk many students do to avoid tardy notices and got to her seat. She chose one in her customary spot at the front of the room.

"Do we have any new students with us this year? asked Mrs. Morton.

There was no response from the class.

"Fine, then," she continued. "Let's talk about our summer writing project, shall we?"

The class let out a muffled groan in unison.

"Oh, now, that's no way to start the year, ladies," said Mrs. Morton, smiling and winking.

"First fiction? Ring any bells? I'm certain you have some wild adventures to share, Miss McMillan."

"We save our wildness for school, Mrs. Morton," replied Cami.

With that, the girls in the class began to laugh instead of moan. It was like Mrs. Morton had a magic wand to cast spells of joy upon a room. There was a knock at the door and she went to answer it. The principal, Sister Beatrice, needed her assistance in the office.

"Go about your studies for other classes, ladies," laughed Mrs. Morton. "I won't be gone long."

As she exited the room, all of the students in Honors English III began chatting amongst themselves. Laura asked Cami if she would join them for study sessions and preparation for the SAT. Her response was an emphatic "Yes!" Celeste introduced herself to a few people at the front of the class, many of whom had never spoken to an African-American girl their own age before. And Becky tried to recruit several students seated near her roost as potential additions—or replacements—for Team BSD.

Ingrid sat silently. To Laura, she had seemed to be in some sort of catatonic shock since Mrs. Morton's class began. It was as if she had transported herself to another time and another place. Laura did not wish to disturb her, though, because she respected all that Ingrid had been through in Belfast. She knew there were still demons in her best friend's mind that had not yet been expelled. Ingrid whispered something under her breath. Laura did not hear her.

"What did you say?" asked Laura.

Ingrid stared blankly ahead at the empty chalkboard.

"Ingrid, what did you say? Are you okay?"

"Enough," whispered Ingrid, barely audible to even her best friend sitting next to her.

"What?" persisted Laura.

"Enough!"

The entire class went silent. All eyes turned to Ingrid, who rose from her seat and began walking to the front of the room. There was a fierce, determined look upon her face. Ingrid turned left in front of Mrs. Morton's desk, then took a direct path to Becky Harken.

"What do *you* want?" blurted Becky.

In a swift motion that would have impressed Bruce Lee, Ingrid Fallon grabbed Becky Harken's ponytail with one hand and slapped her across the face with the other.

"Enough!" screamed Ingrid. "Enough!"

Still pulling on the ponytail, she slapped Becky again.

"You're going to apologize to Celeste right now!" yelled Ingrid. "Do you understand me?"

Becky's face was frozen in fear. She began whimpering, then crying, then balling. Tears were streaming down her cheeks. It had all happened so fast.

"Say it!" screamed Ingrid. "Say it!"

"I'm sorry, Celeste!" cried Becky. "I'm sorry!"

Ingrid let go of the ponytail, but slapped Becky across the face for the third time.

"You're done," said Ingrid calmly. "No one gets bullied by you again. Dumb white bitch."

To say there would never be an incident during the 1981-82 school year at St. Vincent's Academy to eclipse Ingrid Fallon subduing Becky Harken and ending her reign would be wholly accurate. Perhaps this event would *never* be outclassed at any high school in Shreveport, ever.

Ingrid returned to her desk and took her seat. Laura and Cami each put a hand upon her shoulder to comfort her. Celeste got up, walked to Ingrid, and hugged her.

"Thank you," said Celeste. "That is the nicest thing anyone has ever done for me."

Ingrid said nothing. Her breathing had remained calm throughout the attack. She attributed that to the endurance attained on her runs. She sat erect and rested her hands softly upon the desk. Becky put her head upon her own desk and pretended to fall asleep as if she were hibernating. But, she could not hide from her classmates. She could not hide from the past two years of doling out abuse to those she considered weak and frail. Her tears and faint cries were welcomed by the rest of the class. Sarah and Danielle were not able to protect or comfort her this time.

It took about three minutes after the bell rang to end Mrs. Morton's Honors English III class for most of the students at SVA to know that Ingrid Fallon had put the previously feared Becky Harken in her rightful place. That location was with the rest of the mortals at the school, Ingrid and Laura included. Mrs. Morton had given Becky several concerned looks up and down, but no one in the class breathed a word of what had happened. Perhaps their teacher knew this requital was a long time overdue.

Ingrid, Laura, and Cami met Carole and Meredith in the courtyard. Celeste joined them.

"What are you bitches doing this weekend?" asked Carole.

"No plans yet," said Cami. "Football game on Friday night. We'll cook up some trouble, I guarantee it. You in, Celeste?"

"I'm in," answered Celeste, without hesitation.

"I'm free until Sunday morning," said Ingrid.

"I'm in, too," said Laura.

It seemed like every girl in the courtyard at SVA was staring at this convergence and awaiting instructions. Ingrid Fallon had not just championed the cause of Celeste Wilson to correct a past injustice. She had killed the wicked witch.

Cami motioned for Ingrid to join her a few feet away from the group.

"Those slaps were amazing," whispered Cami. "Can you teach me how to do that?"

CHAPTER THIRTY-ONE

"May almighty God bless you, the Father, and the Son, and the Holy Spirit," said Father McQuarters.

"Amen."

It was Sunday, August 30. Father McQuarters looked upon the parishioners as the late afternoon mass at St. Agnes concluded and immediately recognized two familiar faces seated to his lower left. Each wore leather jackets and had herringbone flat caps resting on their thighs. They nodded to Father McQuarters. He nodded back.

—

The station wagon made a sudden stop on a bed of pine needles behind an abandoned shed about 50 yards from the main road. There were cobwebs extended between nearby branches, dirt mounds filled with fire ants, and small swarms of mosquitos. The air was humid as the driver emerged from the vehicle and felt her running shoes land softly upon the moist ground.

Her diary from a summer in Belfast was left behind on the passenger seat.

Checking first to ensure her shoelaces were double-knotted, Ingrid started to run and made her own trail through the trees. She was by herself for the first time since returning to Shreveport. The beating of her heart intensified as she lengthened her strides and quickened her pace.

Ingrid felt invigorated. She embraced the pain of her chest heaving. Each branch that scratched her arms seemed to propel her faster forward. She slipped on wet leaves and bloodied her knees on a large stone. Undaunted, she sprinted further into the forest.

—

Night had fallen in Belfast. A solitary figure emerged from a downtown pub and lit a cigarette. He had begun his morning inside sipping whiskey and now, hours later after several pints of beer, his bearings were disturbed.

The boy heard the clanging of bells from vessels at the nearby docks and smelled the remnants of the day's catch from the sea. There was not a public telephone to be found as he walked into the darkness of a street with abandoned, shuttered buildings.

Ciaran was drunk, lost, and penniless in the city of his birth, but he was not alone.

—

With each stride, Ingrid felt like she was floating above the ground. Her mind was focused on its task and her body was responding. Blood trickled from her knees down to her socks. Each arm looked as it had been whipped with switches. A vine's thorn caught her cheek and left a small cut. She seemed to revel in the misery. She could take the abuse. It would not deter her path.

When one has a broken heart, it is impossible to feel any pain.

Ingrid thought of Cullan and Paddy. She thought of the hunger strikers. She thought about Declan, British soldiers, Father McQuarters, and everything else that had happened to her in Belfast.

And then she thought about Moira.

—

The white van with tinted windows flashed its headlights at Ciaran as it approached him from behind. He turned to look and thought it was a mirage at first, but a friendly hand waved from the passenger side window. Ciaran smiled and walked faster toward it.

There were no other people on the street and no other cars. There was not even a stray, hungry dog to be heard yelping for food. It was just Ciaran in his drunken, hapless stupor and a white van offering a ride on Sunday evening in a Belfast area without street signs.

As Ciaran got closer to the van, the driver turned off its headlights.

—

Ingrid had run several miles without slowing down. Her shoes and socks were wet from mossy puddles and blood. Mosquitos had ravaged her legs. Still, she persevered and repeated the words of Father McQuarters.

You're a brave young woman. You're a brave young woman.

She thought about what took place just a few days ago in Mrs. Morton's class. Ingrid could still feel the burn in her palm from slapping Becky Harken's face three times. She could still feel the strands of Becky's hair under her fingernails. She thought about Celeste's hug and of being at the movies with her, Team CCM, and Laura the night before this run.

Ingrid remembered Moira's words at their picnic together and began to sprint faster.

—

The first shillelagh-like club struck Ciaran directly over the head. The second hit him on the bridge of his nose. It was impossible to count how many punches and kicks were rained down upon him after that.

His limp body was dragged from a nameless street and thrown into the back of the nondescript van. Four men in hoods were his executioners. They attacked him before he even had the chance to scream out for help.

Ciaran had to answer for Paddy. He had to answer for many others, too. The van drove off into the Belfast night and headed for the bountiful countryside of Northern Ireland.

—

Ingrid was able to see glimpses of her destination as she wove in and out of the trees. She had trained for this moment on runs with her father on the grounds of the Norton Art Gallery. She was prepared for the serpentine movements to navigate the thickets and underbrush in the forest. Ingrid felt stronger than she had ever been in her life.

She paused, momentarily, as she saw the water in the distance for the first time. Ingrid bent over to inspect her wounds. She used the sleeve of her shirt to wipe away the acidic sweat causing a burning sensation in her eyes.

He would still be sleeping, she reasoned.

—

Ciaran regained consciousness as he was rolled out of the van onto the softness of the awaiting peat moss. His hands and feet had been bound with twine. His head was hooded. His mouth was taped. His muffled pleas were ignored.

The four men carried him to the banks of a small lake. They affixed weights to his ankles and arms then, without hesitation, pushed him into the water.

Their backs were turned before Ciaran Fallon was completely submerged. He was 17.

—

You're a brave young woman.

Ingrid recalled how helpless she had been when Paddy was attacked. She recalled how helpless she had felt upon learning that something had happened to Moira. She would not be helpless again.

Bloodied, scratched, bitten, torn, and drenched in sweat from a five-mile run through a sweltering Louisiana forest in August, Ingrid arrived at a clearing where she could finally see the lake house.

He would be inside. He would never expect someone to bother him on a Sunday morning.

She got to the driveway and looked at its unfinished wall. Ingrid felt the grains of gravel shift beneath her feet with each step that she took. As in the forest, she felt connected to the earth and at peace. Ingrid began walking toward the lake house.

She stopped, picked up a brick, and continued.

You're a brave young woman.

Clooney would never harm Moira or anyone else again.

CHAPTER THIRTY-TWO (EPILOGUE)

From *Lines of Leaving* by Christy Brown:

Now uncatchable as the wind you go
beyond the wind
and there is nothing in my world
The absurdity of that vast improbable joy.
The absurdity of you gone.

OTHER TITLES BY G.A. CUDDY:

Where Hash Rules
In The Clearing Stands a Boxer
The Grief Poet
The Tao of Pink

Made in the USA
San Bernardino, CA
09 July 2015